VAULTS OF SECRETS

Praise for Vaults of Secrets

Yishau picks a story idea and weaves smaller stories into it that make you almost forget the initial peg, but it works superbly because what unfolds shows just how much a single idea can flow into multiple fascinating pieces. This is arguably art at its best...this work is not easy to put down and clearly shows that the author is a writer who has come to stay.
– Nathaniel Bivan, Daily Trust

If you have ever had secrets, you didn't want people to hear about, that you feel guilty of, that exposes your flaws and imperfections, that you wish never happened, that you wish to be forever buried in obscurity - then Vaults of Secrets is a book you can connect with.

But even if you have no secrets, even if you have been an open book since you were born, it won't hurt to take a peep into the vaults that Olukorede Yishau curates. He offers a master key to these vaults, and his key turns right around and smoothly too as you will find in the pages of this gripping, salacious read.

With stories of infidelity, incest, cultism, murder, politics and so forth, this collection of short stories has the potential of becoming a popular read.
– Nnamdi Oguike, winner, Miles Morland Writing Scholarship and author of Do Not Say It Is Not Your Country

There is a story here for everyone...secrets, regrets, betrayals and many ingredients of human existence...pieced together in simple prose
– Nze Sylva Ifedigbo, author, My Mind Is No Longer Here

Olukorede Yishau 's Vaults of Secrets is a pleasure to read. Its characters invite you to live through their secrets with them... Brilliant stories.
– Ever Obi, author of Men Don't Die

Cute stories. They came out bristling...breathing heavily.
– Edozie Udeze, author of This Wonderful Life

In exploring the capacity of man for duplicity, in his Vaults of Secrets, Olukorede Yishau treats a wide range of subjects that dog the life and death of man. I recommend it. Good job.

– Niran Adedokun, author, The Danfo Driver in Us All

Vaults of Secrets is a collection written with a more serious artistic intent to enable the reader draw some didactic lessons.

Embedded in each story are socio-cultural, economic or political experiences of our time. Just as the late Chinua Achebe said in "the novelist as a teacher" in 'Morning Yet on Creation Day', every author takes up the responsibility to teach some morals by highlighting some of the social contradictions which the society is grappling with. This is exactly what Olukorede S. Yishau has achieved by letting his readers into some of the secrets he keeps in his vaults.

– Chinaka Okoro, The Nation

Vaults of Secrets is a rabbit hole! It drew me in and kept me intrigued with its many twists and turns. Yishau's second book has a peekaboo effect, one moment you think the book is telling you one thing until you realise it just told you something different.

Honestly, I loved the book. It was refreshing to read, a good book of short stories after so many years of shying away from the genre. Yishau has sold short stories to me. I'm all up for reading another collection of short stories.

– Folioreview

Spellbinding narration indeed. In all, the stories are hard to stop reading the moment you start. Great prose.

– Lekan Otufodunrin, Executive Director, Media Career

VAULTS OF SECRETS

OLUKOREDE S. YISHAU

Regium™

Parrésia Publishers Ltd.
82, Allen Avenue, Ikeja, Lagos, Nigeria.
+2348154582178, +2348062392145
origami@parresia.com.ng
www.parresia.com.ng

ISBN: 978-978-56595-7-3

Printed in Nigeria by Parrésia Press

For Titilayo (the one I fondly call Maami) and to the memories of Kayusco (my father) and Sola (my dear sister), who left too early and made me the third born. Also for Funke, Muyiwa, Jide, Bukola, Olumide and Seun.

CONTENTS

1

TILL WE MEET TO PART NO MORE

Oluwakemi,

I remember you today because I saw somebody who bears your name a few minutes ago. The lady is a new addition to our population. Unlike you, she is fair-complexioned. Unlike you, she is plump. Unlike you, she is in here for armed robbery.

She bears no semblance to you, except in name.

I can't remember all the stories and things we talked about, but I remember the day you began to tell me your story; you started with how you met your husband. Because I'm an unrepentant romantic, I concluded the story before you went halfway. She met the man of her dreams, I thought dreamily.

'I met my husband in Queens, New York,' you began. *'I was working at a home for the elderly at the time. In a home such as this, you meet all sorts of aged. Some of them can be so sweet and treat you like their child; some can be outright mean, although this meanness could be tied to a condition. I was in charge of one of the mean ones, an 89-year-old man in the habit of saying awful things. One day, while I was caring for him, he asked me to touch his penis. I refused. He pleaded in a whiny voice and offered me a hundred dollars. I still said no. When he became persistent, I told him I would not touch his*

flaccid, wrinkled penis even if he paid me a thousand dollars, besides that, why would I want to jerk off a man as old as my grandpa. He leered and said he was not old down there. I decided to report him to the male nurse in charge who was also Nigerian. He came to warn the old man. He threatened to have him removed if he did not stop. It turned out this man was notorious for this behaviour even with male nurses. After that incident, the male nurse and I became close and then lovers. It was easy to fall for Jide back then; he wasn't tall or dark with a sharp chin, he was good looking in a specific sort of way and always well dressed. He was warm, he was tolerant of the occupants of the home, but was firm when he had to be, and he was intelligent. Jide was a delight to have a conversation with; we would go on and on about everything under the sun, and always had lots of information, especially about Nigeria. A year and a half later, we got married and decided to return home to Nigeria.

A few years into our marriage, my husband changed. The business he started with our savings from America was not doing well. He became an alcoholic and turned violent; he beat and humiliated me countless times. I wanted to quit the marriage, but I did not; I stayed. I stayed because of our children. I stayed and prayed that he would change.'

I remember that at this point, you stopped and surveyed our dingy cell – you looked left, right and centre as if seeking some secret code embedded within our walls. The story had turned sour, but I somehow knew there was more. I waited.

'One unfortunate day, he came home very drunk and beat me. It had happened many times – he would beat me and punctuate his blows with accusations: I was the reason his fortunes had dwindled. I was the reason he returned to Nigeria. I was the one who did everything, I thought. I was the one who listened to his dreams of how he would make a difference back home. That day, I did something I rarely did - I fought back. I hit him with the first thing I could grip. He fell, and I stood over him, waiting for him to stand so I could hit him again. When minutes later he had not stirred, I bent down to

shake him. That was when I saw the blood flowing from the back of his head.

'I called for help and quickly rushed him to the hospital, where doctors confirmed him dead. Somebody called the police, and they took me into custody. The trial did not take long because I confessed to killing him in self-defence. The judge found me guilty of first-degree murder; his family accused me of killing their son - they said it was premeditated. Nobody mentioned the fact that I had been abused, or that I had been his punching bag, and they had known about it. Here I am, awaiting death. I have been waiting for 15 years, and each day is like torture to me.

'Sometimes, it feels as if the world would consume me. My experience has been one nightmare from which I want to wake up. But it seems I am asking for too much. There is no waking up from this bad dream. The only thing I should look forward to is death, by hanging or old age. If it is by old age, then I still have a long way to go at just 56.

'No one visits me here again. Not my kids; not members of my family. Perhaps, it's because they want to have nothing to do with a killer. I do not blame them; I do not blame myself either. I was only trying to stop a violent man. I could have been the dead one.

'There is something silence does to a condemned person. It makes you contemplate things – you think about all the paths that your life could have taken. I could have been happy; I could have been successful. Maybe I could have been famous.

'My life has been such a drama. Even my childhood was turbulent. I hope I will be able to tell you that story one day.'

You turned away from me and cried silently for the next thirty minutes or so. The tears came at the point you mentioned your turbulent childhood; I wondered what was so traumatic about your childhood that brought tears from your eyes. I did not bother to ask you to stop crying because I was on the verge of tears myself. And I had read somewhere that tears washed the soul and brought healing.

3

That day, as night fell, I thought of how I killed Jacob, my husband who had four other women on whom he was lavishing my money. I didn't kill him with a gun, and no one would have found out if an autopsy had not been carried out. The police discovered a bottle of poison in my house during a sting raid.

I hoped to hear about your childhood someday. I had a fantastic childhood, and I longed to listen to what it felt like to have the opposite.

The day you eventually told me about your childhood, you started with a question: *'Elizabeth, do you know how I got to the United States?'*

I didn't answer yes or no. You had never told me, so I could not know. What I knew, however, was that every time you sprang questions at me out of the blue, it was always a preface to some major revelation. So, I listened.

'My father and mother started it all when they sold me to slavery.'

The mention of slavery sent shock waves down my spine. Slavery? In modern times?

'I was 14 when one day, my father and mother called me and gave me what I thought was great news. A kind woman had offered to take me to the United States, where I would get the best of everything in this world, attend the best schools and fulfil my dreams. I was happy. I was going to enter an aeroplane and go to America. I was excited.

'When Madam Koikoi came to visit, I hardly thought about it when she asked to examine my teeth, asked my parents if I had been ill, and what sort of illness I had suffered from. She asked what class I was in school and wanted to know my best subjects. This happened in our house and my parents were there. After several weeks, I got a passport; then a ticket followed which was neither given to me nor my parents. Eventually, Madam Koikoi informed us she was ready to leave with me to the United States. Every step I took away from our

Ajangbadi home to the airport, up the steps into the belly of the giant bird felt surreal. But I was there in my new clothes, with Madam Koikoi – whom I had now called Aunty – seated beside me, asking me if I was comfortable. After what seemed like an eternity, dotted with the occasional turbulences, the in-flight entertainment as well as bouts of sleep and strict instructions not to talk to anyone as I got up to use the toilet, an air hostess came around asking madam and me to pull up our chairs and fasten our seatbelts because the pilot had announced descent. After a few minutes, a city decorated with what looked like many Christmas lights came into view. The plane landed, its door opened; I was in America. But Madam Koikoi said we were not in America yet. We were in London, and would soon get on another flight to continue our journey. I felt overwhelmed by the travelling.

'Eventually, we got to the U.S. and we took a long taxi ride to Maryland. In Maryland, we passed through areas I never knew could exist. My father told me before I left that the streets of America were paved with gold. That, if I had the opportunity to pick some up, I should, it was free, and I would not be called a thief. Everybody in America was wealthy. We passed neighbourhoods that affirmed that everybody was rich. The houses were huge, had huge spaces between them and no fences, I rubbed my eyes at some point, and aunty laughed when she noticed. "Welcome to the land of milk and honey," she said.

'The first thing Madam Koikoi did when we got to her home in Maryland was to take my passport "for safekeeping". It did not mean anything to me until events unfolded much later.

'Madam Koikoi lived with her husband and a young man introduced to me as her son, although he looked nothing like neither her nor her husband in a big house. But from what I could deduce, Madam Koikoi was the boss of the house. Her husband, a man who seemed younger than she, was not often up and about, except when Madam Koikoi was absent, which was not often. Whenever she was at home, strange noises paraded the house. Sometimes, moaning, sometimes Madam Koikoi just shouting "there… yes, baby, there.

Yes, there …aah… give it to me, give me, give me…" *The noise often seemed like a mixture of crying and screaming joy, and on those days, it went on and on. I did not understand what was happening until I was old enough to know that sexual pleasure could make a woman temporarily mad.*

'A few months after I joined the household, her son left the house. I thought, perhaps, he had gone to a boarding school but I never saw him again and, of course, I couldn't ask. Neither madam nor her husband seemed worried so I let this absence not bother me.

'I had lived in Maryland with madam for almost four years and in those years, I wasn't allowed to go to school, I never went out alone, not even to buy groceries in a supermarket in our neighbourhood. Madam Koikoi told me the police would arrest me and send me to a special prison for black people if they set eyes on me. I hadn't spoken to my parents, in fact, madam said I shouldn't think of them. She said I was to think only of what I would achieve to make them proud when she was eventually ready to teach me.

'My troubles started the day I turned 18. Madam Koikoi called me and told me it was time to start working because I was now an adult. She told me that everyone in America worked. When I asked what work I would do, she gave me a book titled Kamasutra, a book filled with people in various sex positions and asked me to read it. I was disgusted just looking at the pictures, she saw the look on my face and smirked, she then gave me a bigger book that told about sex and self-care. I thought it was a joke. I stared at her in disbelief, but she hissed and walked out of my room. A week after my birthday, she came to my room, slotted a video cassette into the VCR player on top of the television and before my piqued interest could take flight, naked women or barely clothed women and then men floated into focus, what they were doing made me nauseous. Madam Koikoi watched without blinking and occasionally turned to see if my eyes were glued. It made no sense to me, but she was insistent when I tried to protest so we watched tape after tape of Xrated movies. I remember particularly that she asked me to pay attention to the movie Deep Throat.

6

Subsequently, after my first encounter with the movies, she would leave my room.

'Then one day, a few weeks after the visual sexual education and I had come to understand this was the schooling I would receive, she brought a man to my room and asked me to strip. I objected - why would I strip in front of a man, in my room? And why was the man loosening his belt? My question was met with a hard slap across the face. Madam Koikoi ordered me to start doing the things I had watched in Deep Throat to the man. When I resisted, she kicked me and did all sorts of things to break me. She let me rest for some minutes and ordered me to carry out her instructions. I was afraid. But the man told her to leave me alone; he liked his girls feisty. The details of that episode are too painful to repeat. So, I'll just say the man ended up having sex with me and me not with him. It was my first time.

'Sex with strangers became my reality until I was 22. I had learnt that it became easier if I did not resist; I learnt how to use a lube. Different men would come and have sex with me, unprotected and Madam Koikoi was being paid for the service I was providing. I got pregnant on a few occasions until I learnt to protect myself. One day, when Madam Koikoi travelled, Mr Koikoi came to my room and raped me. That was the day I knew why Madam Koikoi screamed in pleasure-pain when she was with him: he had an unusually large phallus.

'I was ashamed and angry. I reported him to Madam Koikoi and they had a nasty fight. Between throwing things at each other and hitting each other with whatever they could find, Madam Koikoi died. Somebody called the police and they came for Mr Koikoi. They took me, too. I told the police the truth and was admitted into a welfare programme run by the state. Through the programme, I got an education and eventually moved to New York, where I met my husband. After a whirlwind courtship, we got married and moved to Nigeria.

'In Nigeria, my father had become famous. He had become rich and close to men in power. However, it was whispered that he was a fraudster; that he duped men of power and famous clergymen. One of them, an Islamic cleric, at the height of his popularity, wanted a yacht. Someone introduced him to my father who sweet-talked the cleric into paying millions. After dropping the money, he was told the money was not enough and was advised to sell some of his exotic cars to pay the difference. The cleric handed over five cars to my father. The cleric never got the yacht, and he never recovered from the loss. He was extremely gullible. It turned out some of the people he knew connived with my father. He died.

'I kept my distance from my father, but I kept abreast of all his activities, especially those reported by the media. I knew about the time he took a chieftaincy title in the East and 'exported' seven musicians from Lagos to perform at the event. The village where the ceremony took place had never seen such opulence before. British pounds sterling and the American dollar were rained endlessly on the musicians.

'But the law eventually caught up with him. In September 2000, at 68, he was arrested by the International Police (INTERPOL), and he ended at the Ikoyi Prison, Lagos. An American, who lost about $10 million to him, was his undoing.

'Of course, he abandoned my mother at the height of his wealth and went about town with small girls on whom he lavished his money. I did not pity my mother because she contributed to my woes. Maybe if she had objected to selling me to a stranger, my life would have taken a different path, and I would not be here in prison. I would not be here to die, like my father.'

Not long after you told me your story, you became ill. We thought it was a minor ailment, and that you would recover, but you worsened with each passing day. One day, after the prison clinic could not handle it, you were taken to a specialist hospital. You did not come back alive. The prison officials told us it was kidney failure.

Before you died, I prayed. I prayed for you because you were a true friend – especially under the circumstances we found ourselves. I prayed and hoped for a miracle. I still remember that Saturday afternoon when I got the news. I had somehow known it but was not quite prepared for it. I shed streams of tears that day. Now, seeing this Oluwakemi, who is nothing like you, is making the tears gather in my eyes again. But, I will not cry; I will be strong as I await my end.

Two weeks after your death, they brought me a new cellmate — Adriana. She was very curious. She asked questions at every opportunity — from me, the warders, from officials of visiting NGOs, and at times, she directed the questions to herself. It looked to me as though she was sick and only her questions could heal her.

One day, I decided to turn the table on her. I asked her question after question. She had answers for them all, but something did not feel right about her. She spoke calmly, eyes unfocused, head bent forward. I let it go. The only thing I believed in her story was that she was in prison because she posed as a madwoman to carry out research in an estate and mistakenly killed a man who attempted to rape her. She was apprehended and a psychiatric evaluation showed that she was normal. The law took its course. After our discussion, I avoided her as much as possible and that made me miss you. I had no one to speak to. There were no deep conversations to make the time here seemingly meaningful — no stories to brighten this present darkness.

Oluwakemi, like you well know, this prison is a house of horror. Here, things that look deep are shallow and shallow things are deep. Many things were going on that we did not know. We did not know that the male warders were raping female inmates. We did not know that sex was used as barter for food, to access the medication your family brought you; to get better living conditions. We did not know that the prison officials were stealing the food we were supposed to eat while awaiting our deaths. We did not know that they were selling them in the open market. I did not know until recently when an inquiry revealed it, and most of the officials in our prison were changed and the people from the Ministry came to visit.

I am sure by now you must have seen Ijeoma, Lillian and Arinola. You were already ill when they passed. Ajara and Ida almost crossed over, but for the quick intervention of the new Prison Chief who used his resources to pay medical consultants.

Oluwakemi, I was dribbling the truth when I said I remembered you because of your namesake. She truly brought you to my mind but the real reason I have decided to write down your story, perhaps my story, in a way, is because I will be with you soon. I have got cancer. Doctors discovered I had Leukaemia shortly after Adriana took your place in the room. I am not bothered and have not cried. Leukaemia has only saved me the hangman's noose or better still; it has saved me the hassle of waiting for a governor who is reluctant to sign my death warrant.

I pray this thing kills me quickly and ends this regular shuttling between the hospital and the prison. I know I deserve to die, but not for killing Jacob. I deserve to die for causing many deaths with the counterfeit drugs I was manufacturing. When my fate comes, I will embrace it.

I'm coming, my dear friend; till we meet to part no more.

2

THIS SPECIAL GIFT

Last Saturday, when Mr Abassima Essien came into my flat looking like all of Lagos was on his shoulders, I knew what he wanted to say before he opened his mouth.

The Saturday before last, I woke up with a terrible cold. It had rained severely for days, and the weather had gotten the better of me, so I stayed indoors. About noon, I saw smoke coming out of the kitchen of the Essiens, my neighbours. I peeped out and saw that Mrs Essien was not around because her car was not in the compound. Quickly, I raced to their flat. I pressed the bell, praying that someone was inside. A fire in the kitchen when the woman of the house was not around is always a deadly thing. No response to the bell. I pressed again; still no answer. I tried to turn the knob and discovered the door was not locked. I opened and ran to the kitchen. The smoke was from a pot on the gas cooker.

I turned off the burner when I found which knob was on and then looked for the cylinder and disconnected it for good measure. With a thick piece of cloth I found, I hurriedly carried the pot over to the sink and opened the tap, water gushed into the pot, moltening whatever had been an intended meal. Eventually, the fire died, leaving smoke in its wake.

I went to the sitting room and sat to catch my breath and regain my strength, all that running around for food that would now not fill a rumbling stomach was energy sapping. Out of curiosity, I climbed the duplex's stairs to see if anyone was home; throughout this whole adventure, no one had run out to see the commotion. There was no one in the only room downstairs where I assumed Idato, the house-help, slept. The first two rooms upstairs were empty too. I wondered if Idato had left the food on fire and stepped out. When I opened the master bedroom's door, I was not prepared for the sight I beheld. Idato, the house-help, and Mr Essien were naked. Idato was doing reverse cowgirl and she saw me immediately I entered and shouted 'Jesus!' The occasions people invite Jesus to!

I dashed out before Mr Essien could know what was wrong. I had barely entered my sitting room when he caught up with me and pleaded that we should enter for him to explain himself.

What was there to explain? He would blame it on the devil, I told myself.

We entered and he launched into his sermon: 'I don't know what got into me.'

I almost laughed. Blame it on the devil, brother! I thought.

'It was the girl. She seduced me and I lost decorum.'

Poor girl. She is not here to defend herself, I thought.

'I promise you this has never happened before, and it will never happen again. The devil is a liar.'

Finally, he used the word, I said. Poor devil, every sinner's fall guy.

I was short of words and simply told him I had heard, like I always do when my gift rears its head. I have this special gift, of walking in at the wrong time. Like walking in on colleagues making out in the office shortly after closing time. Like walking in on a senior colleague shredding documents to cover up fraud. Like seeing a man I know very well being intimate with a mentally-challenged woman. Like stumbling on the fact that my pastor has a child outside wedlock.

Thirty minutes after Mr Essien left my apartment, I saw Idato bearing a Ghana-must-go bag and leaving the compound. Did he ask her to leave? Was it her decision? I had no way of knowing. I felt that Mr Essien wanted to conceal his secret. I had no way of confirming that, either.

One week later, last Saturday, Mr Essien was back in my apartment, pleading with me not to ever mention his dirty little secret to his wife.

'It will destroy our relationship. She has so much trust in me. If they hear this thing in the church, it will destroy me,' he pleaded.

I looked at him and wondered why he had to go through so much pain trying to cover his tracks. With me, secrets are always safe. I have vaults where I keep them.

Mr Essien's misadventure brought a brother to my mind. This brother is not a friend who I call a brother, not a christian brother from church, but my brother who has known me my entire life and knows more about me than any other person. My brother did not tell me any secret, I chanced on it. This is how it happened. Shortly after we completed his house in Ikeja, he came home from Cape Town. I went to see him after the initial celebrations. I had called to tell him I was coming, so he met me in the sitting room. He seemed hurried and wanted us to go out for beer and goat meat pepper-soup. I was excited, until I saw a woman walking down the stairs.

I recognised the woman immediately. It was Oyebola, the mother of my brother's three older children, who abandoned him when things were rough. My brother ran to the stairs leaping two stairs at a time to reach her. They spoke in hushed voices for a few minutes then she went back up. He came back down stairs.

'Now you know,' he said.

'Know what?'

'Stop the pretence, please. Just promise me Jane will not know.'

Jane is my brother's wife in Cape Town. She too has three children by him. She picked him up from the gutter where Oyebola dumped him and dressed him up in designer clothes. The house, in which Oyebola came majestically down its stairs like she owned it, was built with Jane's money. 'You can't expect me to abandon the woman who has three boys for me. Jane has only girls.'

'Oh,' I said, 'and girls are not children?'

'Look, spare me. Just promise me you'll keep this to yourself. You are my only brother and we have lost both parents so you must have my back.'

I said nothing.

'So, are we still going for the beer and pepper-soup?'

'Let's go,' I said.

I remember another secret I regret keeping, to this day.

It was a Friday. I had just come out of the cinema at the Novare Mall in Sangotedo where I had gone to see *Alakada Reloaded* when my phone rang and the caller ID showed that it was my boss, Nonso, whose name instilled fear into top bankers, A-list politicians and every other who-is-who with skeletons in their cupboards.

He asked me to see him by 9pm. Looking back now, I wish I'd found an excuse not to see him. If I had not seen him, I would not have become the hostage of a secret which destroyed my best friend.

I checked my watch and saw that I could make it to Banana Island the time he asked me to see him.

As I made my way to the expansive car park of this beautiful mall some forty minutes away from the Island town of Epe, the image of my controversial boss filled my head.

Nonso, heavily-built and with a protruding belly that made it difficult for him to wear a pair of shoes on his own, was a man of questionable character. He had been a politician in the aborted Third Republic. His foray into publishing after being a politician gave him the leverage that only a few publishers had. Many feared his newspaper, *This Country*, rather than respect it. The fear of Nonso was the beginning of wisdom for business people and politicians. Bank executives worshipped the ground he walked on and paid good money for his favours. Nonso got paid piles of money for adverts in advance, but it all went to support his lavish lifestyle.

Nonso could lease a jet to fly to the UK to suck a girlfriend's breasts. He could camp a girl in Eko Hotel for weeks so she could fiddle with his penis. He was a perfect example of what success should not be. But in an abnormal clime like Nigeria, Nonso was a kingmaker, a man to be reckoned with if one wanted to secure his ascent or upturn the progress of others.

Paying staff salaries was not Nonso's priority. There were instances when staff down-tooled and he quickly paid them, but he always found a way of hitting back. He was fond of telling reporters that he knew they were using his newspaper's identity card to make money. And to top that, Nonso was reputed for wanting the same women his employees wanted. His liaison with the wife of one of his former editors led to the collapse of the editor's marriage. When he attempted to export his business model to London and South Africa, it ended in calamity. His assets were sold off in South Africa to pay the workers he owed.

I wondered why he wanted to see me. Of recent, I had been

lukewarm about my job and if my plans had worked, I would have relocated abroad.

I made my way out of the mall in my green Toyota Corolla 2005 model after dropping the tally number with a guard who said 'have a good evening' as if he was saying 'find me something for the weekend'.

The traffic was smooth all the way to Victoria Garden City, but when I got to Ikate-Elegushi, my car was stuck on one spot for 27 minutes. Hawkers made brisk business selling bottled water, sachet water and soft drinks. Beggars too had a field day canvassing for alms. I could see many in commercial vehicles sweating out their frustration. The clog of yellow-rusted buses hooting their horns added to the confusion on the Lekki-Epe Expressway. It was a tug of war passing through Circle Mall, and hell escaping into Lekki Phase 1.

The hordes of young people usually soliciting for customers shortly after the Lekki Phase 1 second gate had cleared out because the Canada Visa Centre, which they served, had closed by the time I got there. Five hours earlier, when I passed through the gate, tens of young men had besieged my car, asking if I wanted a passport photograph or needed photocopying. They had a way of assuming everyone at that spot was trying to leave the country.

After passing Dr. Tony Rapu's church called THIS PRESENT HOUSE, I ran into another traffic jam caused by the toll gates on the beautiful Lekki-Ikoyi Bridge. Vehicles moved at snail's pace, and street hawkers were not in short supply. From handkerchiefs to potato chips to Tom-Tom, all were on sale. One could even buy knives and cutlasses.

My attention was drawn to a couple in a Range Rover Evoque; the glasses were wound up, and I could not hear what they were saying, but it was clear they were in a heated argument. The man slapped the woman, got out of the car and started walking away. The poor woman, who obviously could not drive, sat there crying while other drivers honked around her. I found my way out and quickly moved towards the gates. Five minutes later, I was paying the N300 toll fee, collecting my receipt from the smiling female attendant and zooming off into Ikoyi. I checked the time. It was 8.31pm. I smiled, sure that I would be on time for my appointment with my boss in his Banana Island residence.

Soon I was on Onikoyi Road, the gateway to Banana Island. I cruised past the Redeemed Christian Church of God, where Professor Yemi Osinbajo pastored before becoming the vice-president. At the first gate, I was asked who I wanted to see.

'Mr Nonso Ejiofor,' I said.

They asked for my name and what followed showed that Nonso had given them my name as a guest. I was given a password, 'giraffe', which I would tell those at the second gate before they would allow me to proceed to Abia Street.

The Island reeked of wealth: well-laid out road network, well-mowed lawn, perfumed air, well-built and glossed mansions and an ambience comparable to Seventh Arrondissement in Paris, La Jolla in San Diego and Tokyo's Shibuya and Roppongi.

There were no pot-holes, no house with peeling paint; no form of shabbiness had room in this rich's playground.

I was in front of Airtel's headquarters when my phone buzzed. It was a text from Nonso; it read: 'Wait for me, I will soon join you.'

It was a confirmation the man was not at home and I would have to wait. Waiting for Nonso was not a strange thing. His editors always waited for his authorisation every day before going to bed. There were times they would have finished production and patted themselves on the back for a job well done and he would tear apart all they had done. He would ask the editor on duty to take a pen and he would dictate what would lead the paper for the following day. A former editor once told me that Nonso always made him feel like he was just a figurehead.

As I drove around, I wondered which house was Mike Adenuga's and which was Sayyu Dantata's. I noticed that on the residential side, there were no four-storied buildings. I drove past Ocean Parade Towers, a series of 14 luxury tower blocks, and wished I could own a piece of it.

The bliss on the Island did not prepare me for the storm to come. By 10pm, I was still outside Nonso's imposing white mansion. I was getting sick and tired. Something told me to call Nonso's bluff and head home. After all, Saturday was my work-free day. But another voice asked me to wait it out. I was later to understand that it was my special gift at work!

In the house opposite Nonso's place, the garage boasted a Rolls Royce Phantom, Bentley Continental, a Ferrari, Range Rover and Porsche 911. I wondered who owned the house and why he needed all these luxury cars. I imagined that the person must have a private jet parked at a private hangar in Ikeja. I imagined the owner inside the house holding a champagne flute from which he sipped copiously.

I took myself inside Nonso's mansion, mentally. I imagined that the furniture would be imported; I imagined some domestic hands doing one chore or the other. I was sure there would be no kids or wife because they all lived abroad. I imagined the living room would be massive—like Nonso. I wondered what would be going on in the kitchen because Nonso ate out most of the time. I wondered if Nonso liked his life or if he was not in control of it any longer. My attention was diverted when around 11pm, my phone rang. It was Nonso again.

'Come to Eko Signature. Tell the receptionist you want to see me,' he said and hung up before I could complain.

This man must be mad, I said to myself, took a deep breath, exhaled and began to drive out of the well-lit road of Banana Island. The roads were no longer busy, so in less than ten minutes, I was standing at the reception of Eko Signature, the latest addition to the Eko Hotels and Suites. I admired the imposing reception area, the bar, the lights, the wood panels on the wall and the giant-rolling door that let me in.

After I was cleared to go up to see Nonso, I dashed to the elevator and an attendant, obviously called by the chubby-cheeked, fair-complexioned beauty who was the receptionist, followed me. I tried to operate the elevator, but with no success. The attendant looked at me and smiled as though saying this must be a Johnny Just Come.

'You can't access the elevator or any floor here without us or a guest letting you in; that is why it is called Signature. You can't enter without the signature,' he said and brought out a card, pressed it somewhere near the elevator and it opened. A minute later, I was inside Nonso's suite.

'How are you?' Nonso said. He was in a pair of shorts. His beer-belly was uncovered, his feet bare and his grey hair uncombed. I returned his greetings and could immediately smell the presence of a female. And just before we could start any discussion, a young woman, probably 22, walked out of the room, shouting 'Nonso, Nonso'.

I felt like the ground would open and consume me. How could this girl call someone old enough to be her father by his first name?

'Good evening sir,' the girl said to me and I was infuriated. Nonso had sold his honour to the girl. I still had mine.

The voluptuous girl walked back into the room, leaving Nonso and me in the sitting room. I looked forward to hearing why Nonso called me.

"Emmanuel —"

Nonso's phone rang and he held the phone to me. 'Sorry, this is Okowa calling.' He picked the call and said: 'Your Excellency. Good evening, sir.' He listened. 'Thank you, your Excellency. To what do I owe the honour of this call?'

For reasons I could not understand, Nonso put the call on speaker. Perhaps he wanted me to confirm that he was truly speaking with the Delta State governor.

'We are holding this economic summit in Asaba and I want you to chair the occasion,' the governor said.

'That should not be a problem. Tell your boys to send me the details by mail and I will be there live and direct,' said Nonso.

'You will have the details first thing tomorrow morning. Good night, my brother,' the governor said.

'Good night, your Excellency.'

Immediately he dropped the call, another of his phones rang. He told me later that the call was from a bank MD who wanted some editorial favours.

'That is a small thing, but you know how it goes,' Nonso said quietly, before bursting into a guffaw.

'All right then,' Nonso said and added: 'Good night, my brother.'

The girl soon came out again to whisper something into Nonso's ear and he burst out laughing. I felt like standing up and slapping the girl for not staying inside until we were through with the business at hand.

'Will you like to go to London?' Nonso asked, catching me unaware.

'Yes sir,' I said without thinking.

'It is for a conference. You will get the details tomorrow.'

The door opened again, and I assumed it would be the bosomy girl; it was not. Walking into the sitting room from the same bedroom the small girl entered was Dunni, my best friend's wife of five months.

Like me, Dunni was shocked but summoned the courage to come and whisper to Nonso. She greeted me as though we were meeting for the first time. I played along. She went back in and Nonso dismissed me by saying: 'I have urgent and pressing national matters to attend to inside.'

I didn't allow myself to think about what three people would be doing in one room. I knew what a threesome was, and I knew that it was not one of my fantasies. What bothered me more, however, was: What kind of married woman got involved in a threesome with an older man and a slip of a girl? What kind of woman did my best friend marry?

It was way past midnight when I sped through the Third Mainland Bridge and went home to my apartment in Mende, Maryland.

Sleep did not come easily that day. Ozolua and I had spoken earlier, and he had told me that Dunni was out of town for a conference. That night Dunni sent me a WhatsApp message pleading with me not to tell Ozolua. Nonso, she said, was an old benefactor who insisted on seeing her one last time. I did not respond.

A week later, I flew out to London. As is typical, friends saddled me with a list of what they wanted me to get for them. Ozolua drove me to the airport, and Dunni came along saying she wanted to see Uncle Emmanuel off.

As the two of them held hands and gave me a joint hug at the departure hall, I was tempted to drop some hint to my friend, but I did not want to break a home. That day, as my flight took off and Lagos gradually became smaller and turned into a map, I knew that my tongue would remain fettered. My silence had made me complicit. I would never be able to speak about the issue. If I ever did, I would be accused of having evil intentions.

I was still in London when Ozolua called me. I could barely hear him because he sounded broken and angry.

'Dunni is a damned cheat, a fucking liar,' he said.

'Ozo baba, what's going on?'

'What's going on? My wife has been shagging your boss!'

'What!? How did you know?' I said. Internally, I was happy that the truth was out, and it didn't come from me. But I was curious to know how.

'The police called me this morning to say she was at Bar Beach Police Station. She and another lady were found in a hotel room with your chairman, dead.'

I was lost for words. I was disappointed in Dunni. So, she returned to Nonso, and so quickly too.

'I'm sorry,' I said.

He went on to tell me she would be charged to court soon. For manslaughter? For culpable homicide? He was not sure. On my part, I felt responsible for my chairman's death. I also knew that things would change at our newspaper company.

It's been three years since Chairman's death. Dunni and the other lady, who I suspected to be the small girl at Eko Signature, are out free because Chairman's family said they were not interested in washing their dirty linen in public. This came after the autopsy showed that Chairman died of a sudden heart attack.

Ozolua has found it difficult to trust another woman. I have tried to convince him that Dunni does not represent the female population. My sermonising that there are still good women falls on deaf ears. He says once bitten a thousand times shy.

Now, each time I am with him, I feel bad about that one moment when my tongue should have refused to be fettered. But I also wonder what would have happened if I told him what my special gift had led me to discover.

3

MY MOTHER'S FATHER IS MY FATHER

Dear diary,

Let me narrate my dreams and my reality. Let me say it as it is.

It seems like it's going to rain. My grandfather is seated beside me in the car. We are on a long stretch of road, going to nowhere.

'I'm sorry,' he says.

I look at him, puzzled. Why is he sorry?

'I'm sorry,' he repeats.

The rain is finally here. It descends in heavy sheets, pounding the body of the car in a steady rhythm. I turn on the wiper and look at my grandfather.

'I'm sorry,' he coos, placing his hand on my right hand on the steering.

Suddenly, the rain stops, as if someone has turned off a switch. Our vast surroundings bear no testament of the downpour. At once, I start having the feeling that something is taking over my body.

Grandfather places his second hand on my left hand, and I slip out of my body as my grandfather occupies it.

The eyes and the visage of my body are as I have always known them – mine. But the essence, myself, has gone out of it. I hear my grandfather in my body telling me to understand; telling me we are one. I hear him say there is a job he has to do, and it can only be done with my body. I hear everything he is saying, I can't speak. I know what I want to say, but when I try to speak no sounds come out.

'I offended you, I offended your mother; I offended your grandmother. Even God is unhappy with me.'

He urges me to pray for him to receive God's favour, Grandma's forgiveness and my mother's clemency. I crave the freedom to tell him that his sin, whatever it is, is forgiven. I want to become my mother, my grandmother and God, and grant him the peace he so badly wants. But I can make no sounds, no matter how I try.

Then, suddenly, it seems like something begins to call my name, begins to nudge me softly but rhythmically. In a flash, I am back in my body. But it seems like something is sucking me in; sucking the life out of me. I open my mouth to scream. I can't hear myself, so I scream louder to stop life from draining out of me.

Jesus Christ! I shout and roll off my hotel room bed to the floor, I land with a dull thud. I am sweating. This is the seventh time this month I am having a dream featuring my father-grandfather.

Now that my father-grandfather visits me in my dreams regularly, my wife has been worried. Not because she knows anything but because I have cried out of my sleep at least three times while she is beside me. She has suggested that I see her pastor, but my trust in men of the cloth is weightless. Besides, I know what the issue is and will find a way out.

I am one of those people who have no right to protest if called a product of ignominy.

Apart from me, no one else alive knows. I am happy that my secret is guarded and I hope to keep it so till I breathe my last. I am only recording it here for posterity's sake.

26

My mother, Evelyn Ababio, lied about not knowing who my father was. The Ababio I bear is her father's name. What my mother could not tell me was that her father is my father; that she is my mother and my sister. Everybody in our little house knew – my mother, her mother, and of course my father-grandfather. But shame hardly ever bows to truth, except when forced. They think I do not know, but I do. I know that the story that my mother was raped is a lie. I know that the tale that the rapist was never found is another lie. I know that the story that my mother could never marry because of what had happened to her was almost the truth; but it was truth born to protect the truth – an alternative truth.

The first time my father-grandfather appeared in my dreams, I asked him about his dual role in my existence and all I got was silence. 'Some things,' the silence said, 'are better left unsaid.'

How did I find out about my father who is also my grandfather? It was in 1969. I was about to begin school and it was required that I come with my father. Grandpa chose to go with me. I felt no awkwardness because Grandpa had always been the father I knew. The one who sired me, I had been told, could not be traced.

When we returned home after the registration, I stayed back in the sitting room while Grandpa went into my mother's room to brief her about how it all went. Some minutes later, my mother came out of the room and sent me to the market. She asked me to get seasoning and condiments from her regular stall. At the stall, all I ever needed to do was to give the store owner money, and she knew what to give me.

That day, I ran all the way to and from the stall because I wanted to tell my mother what the school was like and that I could not wait to go there every day. When I returned, I heard loud voices. Grandma's voice over-rode them all. It was not too loud, but it was sharp; its tone strident.

As I made to enter the passage, I heard Grandma say, 'Useless man.' I stood rooted to the spot. Why was Grandma addressing Grandpa in that manner? Why did he not say anything? Why was my mother sobbing? I was afraid.

Before I could recover from the shock, Grandma's voice came again. 'I regret the day I met you. All your mates were able to give their wives plenty children. You were able to give me only one and what did you do with her life? You shattered it. Almost every man in this village has accused you of leering at their wives. The seeds that you were supposed to give me to make children were wasted outside, and you always returned home with remnants – seeds that were too tired to sprout. And because you are unfortunate, the next time your seed decided to take root, it was on your daughter.' I was shocked. I imagined Grandma was on her feet, her hands clapping softly in Grandpa's face. I imagined that Grandpa was seated, head bowed. I imagined mother seated on a low stool, her wrapper gathered into her laps, sobbing.

Grandma had not finished. 'You just could not control that snake between your legs. It dragged you into your daughter's thighs, and the product is Williams.'

I almost passed out. So, it was on my body that the fart smelled. Tears welled up in my eyes and cascaded down my cheeks. I was about to clean my face and go inside when I heard my mother's voice. Her teary voice broke my heart.

'Baba, you brought me to this world and it was you who destroyed me. That day, Baba, you were not drunk. Your eyes were clear. You simply walked into my room and locked the door and ordered me to remove my blouse. I thought you were going to rub some medicine on my body, as you had done in the past when I had a fever. I did not suspect you, Baba, I did not. But when you began to pull my skirt, I asked what you wanted to do; you asked me to shut up. You said you were trying to save me and I was being head-strong. I was 19 and a virgin. You violated me and my life has never been the same,' my mother said.

When Grandpa spoke, his barely audible voice was broken. All I could hear him say was that he was sorry. He called my mother by name and pleaded with her. He called Grandma by name and begged her. He stressed the fact that I must never know and pleaded with my mother and Grandma to keep me away from the shameful past.

When I had heard enough, I went to the village square. After some minutes in the square, I became bored and decided to take a tour of the village. Taatuu, our small village, was an assemblage of mud houses, many were varnished in such a way that they could be easily mistaken for brick houses. The rich people were mainly farmers and fishermen who took advantage of our closeness to the river to fish and irrigate their farmlands.

As I walked around the village, tears welled up in my eyes. My young mind was in turmoil. I had grasped the import that there was something shameful about my being. I eventually got tired of the tour and returned home to face the three people in my life who had chosen to make my life a lie. But as a child, I could not confront them. I just lived the lie and moved on; after all, anger against one's blood is felt on the flesh, not in the bone.

Not long after Grandpa's secret became known to me, he died. He was not sick. He just slept and did not wake up. Five years after, Grandma too passed on. I was left with only my mother. She toiled day and night for me to become somebody in this life. But just as I was admitted into the university, she vanished.

She had a fever, got better and decided to take a stroll. She never returned home. We searched and searched, but she was never found.

I thought my end had come. My case was like that of a man looking for a wife at the time the market was filled with mad people. When I started to accept the truth that my mother was not coming home, I also felt relieved. All the people who knew about my conception had gone to the grave with the secret. And me, I would not go to university.

Not long after the disappearance of my mother-sister, a prominent son of our village came home from abroad. My plight was brought to his knowledge, and he decided to take me as his son. One month after, we left together for London, where I had my tertiary education at the London School of Journalism.

London welcomed me in the evening. Thanks to a fantastic Nigeria Airways flight in which I slept all through the six hours. I slept more out of fright than any other thing. It was my first flight, local or international.

The London I arrived in was where pensioners outside Margaret Thatcher's home bore placards with inscriptions, such as 'Give us back our fuel allowance' and 'Help the needy, not the greedy'. The Margaret Thatcher conservative government, which emerged in 1979, was letting go of government-run industries which the Tories felt were costing more to run. And many resisted.

The LSJ campus on Shirland Road was a beehive when I got there for resumption formalities. The image of British novelist Sir Max Pemberton, who founded the college in 1920, loomed large as I walked from one office to the other to regularise my studentship.

LSJ, as we fondly called it, taught me how to be the best in creative writing and journalism. But my memory of London transcended LSJ. It was in London that I met Alake, who was the goddess that guided me for the large part of my stay in London.

The first time I met Alake Balogun, a student like me, was at a bar near Wembley Stadium. It was the day protesters in London marched against Apartheid in South Africa. The streets of London in those days were filled with punks, record shops and rock stars.

The bar had a coffee shop where Alake was before I got there. She was having a debate with the coffee section's attendant about racism and its implications. I listened as she condemned all forms of segregation and vowed to resist any attempt to make her a second class citizen.

I was taken aback by this 'white' girl and her talk about being a second-class citizen. Alake looked every inch British. She looked Caucasian but proudly told everyone that she was a Nigerian. When I got to know her, I found out that her mother, a Briton, had met and married a Nigerian student in the mid-60s. Clearly, Alake inherited all her mother's genes.

That evening, when Alake and I got talking, she was excited to see someone from home. She had been in London since she was six. Though born in Liverpool, she lived in Lagos for about five years.

We became acquaintances and regularly took the tube from Oxford Circus, Marble Arch, Tottenham Court Road, Leicester Square, Bond Street, Charing Cross and Piccadilly Circus. Most times, we had no particular destination. Alake was just interested in showing me the city.

Alake and I were witnesses to the changes in the London skyline. Architectural masterpieces, such as the Natwest Tower and the Barbican Centre, sprang up and we were there to bask in the euphoria. We were at Dingwall's Club to see The Smiths. We went to shows upon shows, including the one by Madonna at Camden Palace in 1983. By the time we went for the Madonna show, Alake and I had crossed the line of friendship; we had become lovers.

Alake and I held our relationship for one year until she started treating me coldly. The first day I noticed her coldness was at a restaurant on Beck Road, where I had invited her. I waited for about an hour before she showed up. When she came, she apologised brusquely and I wondered what the matter was. After that dinner, seeing her became a problem. I went to her apartment near the West Brompton Station repeatedly for weeks but I didn't see her. I hung around a library she used to frequent at Dalston, but I did not find her either.

No friend could tell me where Alake was. So, I took solace in my studies and spent a lot of time reading classics by Tolstoy and Dostoevsky. I added a second companion, Vodka.

One night I went to a club around Oxford Street, had more than my fair share of drinks and woke up the next morning in the arms of a stranger. Before I could make sense of where I was, the girl called me Sweet and said she enjoyed our lovemaking. I could not remember the details. I left the place, the girl having emptied my wallet. That night was the first time father-grandfather came to me in my dreams. I also saw Alake and she was running away from my father-grandfather. I tried to run after her, but she kept pointing in the direction of father-grandfather and increasing her pace.

I came to the end of my studies in London and returned home a day after Bob Geldof of the Boomtown Rats, and some other bands organised the Live Aid Concert at Wembley using the song 'Do They Know It's Christmas?' to raise money for the poor in Africa.

Back home, I started living a relatively comfortable life in Lagos. Thanks to a good job in a multinational company's corporate communications unit. For years, I was not interested in pursuing a serious relationship. I was interested only in Alake, my lost love. I often wondered what happened: Did she find out about me? Did my father-grandfather appear to her? I had so many questions and no answers to them. The fact was that Alake had gone. Like the dew that was present in the early morn and gone before the sun rose, she was no longer a part of me.

Alake became, for me, a muse, and poetry became my lover. I wrote piles and piles of poetry for Alake my lost angel. For me, poetry began and ended with Alake, my runaway lover. I knew at the time that I risked sounding monotonous, but I was writing for no one but myself and my Alake. But what could have happened? Did she find out, but how could she? Did a spiritualist tell her about my past? Did my father-grandfather visit her too? These questions bugged me until I accepted there would be no Alake and I forever.

I eventually met and married Omolola, and we have two children. To my wife, I was simply an orphan at the time we met. I did not think I needed to go into how I came to be. The details are too sordid to be told. Plus, the circumstances of my birth are mine to bear, alone. Thankfully, orphans have no family ties and so I did not need to take her 'home' or introduce her to extended family. I was without roots.

It is dark and father-grandfather and I are on the road again. This time, we are on a road I know like the back of my palm. We are on Allen Avenue. I can see Mike Adenuga's building, which plays host to Glo's office. Not far from it is a house, which used to belong to a fraudster. We are parked and some girls are trying to get our attention. One of them comes closer and runs away, screaming as though she has seen a ghost. Father-grandfather laughs. I don't know why and simply keep mum.

He begins to talk to me; to tell me about things that mean nothing to me. He tells me about walking in God's path to have eternal life. He talks about rejecting vanity and not joining the rat race. He talks about anything that catches his fancy.

Soon a guy comes to our car and shoots at father-grandfather. His bullet does not penetrate. He tries again. Still no luck. When he aims at me, I scream and wake up.

For the first time in a long while, I open my Bible and pray. I tell God to drive all my afflictions away. I beg Him to fight anyone fighting me. I beseech Him to set me free.

The next day I have no nightmare. The next day, nothing; the day after that, I sleep soundly. Fourteen days in a row, I sleep without dreaming. By this time, I am back home and each night, I pray that it is truly over.

On the third night after I return home, Omolola and I have celebratory coitus to mark the end of my nightmares. That night, the dream returns and I scream back to life. When my wife asks me what the problem is, I tell her not to worry. She advises me to stop lying on my back. She says she notices I have the nightmare when I sleep that way.

'Sleep on either side or on your stomach,' she advises.

Surprisingly, she does not talk about seeing a prayer contractor. I continue to pray and follow her advice. Anytime she notices I am sleeping on my back, she nudges gently, 'Darling, adjust yourself.'

For two months, my dreams are clean. Each night before going to bed, I kneel by my bedside and pray. Then I lie dutifully on my stomach or side. The fear of nightmares becomes the beginning of wisdom for me.

My joy is cut short, as father-grandfather returns to my dreams, and this time with my mother who is also my half-sister. As the dreams begin to seem more real and the screams become more intense, I wonder if it is time to reveal a part of me unknown to others.

4

LETTERS FROM THE BASEMENT

We did not see it coming.

We had a good life – Okwy and I, and our children. We were on top of the world until I was shown that only God could not be abased.

Nothing prepared me for my time at the Basement Maximum Prison. When I was funding treasonable acts against my country, I thought my tracks were well covered. Until the law caught me. Red-handed. Since then, this tiny room has been my home. The security post at the Government House is better than this; the servant quarters in my personal house are mansions compared to this.

Okwy's letter from Accra arrived the day I got a roommate. This prison, half of it underground, has a way of giving condemned prisoners like me some preferential treatments as if the authorities want us to have some good times before facing the hangman's noose.

One of such luxuries was the private room, with basic amenities. We were also allowed visitors once a month. Once a month could become every day if our visitors could grease palms generously. Unfortunately for me, I was alone. All the people I had sowed my political capital had deserted me.

Okwy's letter, which the officials had opened and read before bringing to me, was a soothing balm. I was glad to read from my darling wife, whom I had caused many pains.

My Dear Nelson,

I don't know how to begin this letter. Please understand the circumstances surrounding my writing it. Victor and Blessing send their greetings from Accra.

The last few months have been hell without you. The children and I are extremely sad at the turn of events. It is painful how our lives which had been blooming and glowing for years, wilted in a matter of months.

The children have started school here. I decided to enrol them in school here the day you were convicted because I knew I could not return to Nigeria anytime soon, with the way things turned out.

I cry almost every night. I am sure my pillow must be tired of my tears and soliloquy by now. There are times I feel I am losing my mind, but I am keeping it together, because of our children. They need me now that you are not here.

By the time you are reading this, my boutique and unisex salon would have started operations here in Ghana. I decided to start this business from the money you gave me before you hustled us out of the country. I pray that the salon works and pays our bills. We have minimal bills these days because I have learnt to cut down on the things we don't need.

If miracles still happen, you should be out of prison soon because I wish and pray for a miracle every day. Ghana, like Nigeria, is a deeply religious country, and I have taken advantage of this so as not to lose my sanity. I believe you'll be released because I have made sacrificial offerings and prayers so that you can be free again.

My dear husband, you cannot imagine the number of times I have paused while writing this letter to cry and mourn the nonsense that our lives have become.

Blessing and Victor have stopped asking me about your chances of freedom.

They stopped asking after I could not answer a question Victor asked after reading an article from a Ghanaian website. Mummy, did Daddy really do it? *He asked. I have avoided variants of this question or tried to explain that incarceration was one of those things that happened to people in politics in Nigeria. But, my husband, the day our son printed that article and brought it home, I could not say anything. All the facts of the case and your sentencing were there. It was titled* NIGERIAN EX-GOVERNOR TO HANG FOR TREASON. *That day, since my silence, they too have gone silent. They have carried on living their lives, and I am worried.*

My father is dead. He died, and I could not attend his funeral because it happened in the heat of your trial. Thankfully, Alice and her husband were there to make sure that things went well. From what Alice told me, father suffered in his last moments. He'd been battling with prostate cancer and in his final moments, he was in pain. I wasn't at his side, but I hope his spirit will let me rest. I did my best when I could, like a good daughter. I also did my bit as a devoted wife by standing with you in trials.

I miss you; I miss your touch. I hope you'll understand this. I am a woman still in my prime. There were nights I woke up suddenly and wished you were beside me. I craved for your skin on mine; I craved for the passionate rhythm we felt together. In those moments, my body quaked with yearning with no one to fulfil them. I cannot begin to tell you the things I have learnt to deal with such situations. It has not been easy, dear husband.

I will continue to pray for you and will write to you again. I will come to see you when it is safe to do so. I love you; I will always do.

Be strong.

Your Okwy.

I was emotionally down by the time I finished reading the letter. I also wondered why the prison official did not allow Okwy's sister see me when she brought the letter. Or did she send someone to bring it? Was she ashamed to see me? I stopped thinking about it. The options that presented themselves were dire.

I got hold of myself and decided to reply Okwy and have it posted to Accra for me by a pliant officer.

My Okwy,

You may never know how glad I was to read from you. Though the contents of your letter made me sad, knowing that you are doing well has lifted my spirit and further strengthened me to wait for whatever is coming.

Let me first thank you for shouldering the responsibility for two and for being strong about it. It was very thoughtful of you to start the boutique and salon business. My money in Nigeria that you could have fallen back on has all been taken over by the government. The court ruled that all my properties and cash should be forfeited to the government on account of funding terrorism. So, it was wise of you to have used your initiative and moved on.

It was touching to read about how you have been unable to cheat nature. I am so sorry about that. Please find a space in your heart to forgive me. I did not know it will end this way when I decided to fund them. I maintain that I felt that I was working for the greater good when I agreed to fund those activists. Please, do whatever you need to do to sate your sexual urge. It pains me to write this, but I have to be fair to you; what choice do I have?

I, too, have missed your touch. I have missed your encouragement; I have missed your compassion. And the kids, how I long to see them! Your news about their silence hurts me. But please, find a way to break through their reticence. Do what you can to know exactly what's going on with them.

The prison allows us to receive visitors once in a month, the last Saturday of every month. It will be good to see you guys.

Once again I am sorry for the mess I have put you through. Please forgive me and do come to see me with the children.

Your Nelson.

The letter was dispatched, and I waited for a reply. Weeks passed one after the other, and when they became a group, they turned into months. A month, two months, three months… It was almost four months before a letter came. It was borne by Okwy's sister who came to see me.

It was handwritten in Okwy's beautiful cursive. I recalled a time when her cursive only appeared on scented paper.

My Dear Nelson,

I am sorry I am just writing to you. My late response is due to circumstances beyond my control. I am grateful to God that I can even write you now.

The day after your letter was delivered, Blessing woke up in the morning with pains in her abdomen. I asked her what she ate, but she said nothing. Within minutes, the pains became unbearable for her and I rushed her to the hospital. That is where we have been all these weeks.

Nelson, Blessing was having an affair with a man twice her age. Yes, you read, right. Our sixteen-year-old daughter became pregnant for a thirty-three-year-old man. The man, instead of telling her that he did not want the baby, deceived her that he would come to us and do the right thing. But he was secretly poisoning her to terminate the pregnancy. He was giving her what she thought was juice, not knowing that he mixed in concoctions that could kill the foetus and kill her too. It took tests upon tests to discover because Blessing did not think that what was wrong with her could have come from her lover. Doctors had to ask her questions before we could resolve the puzzle.

We sent the police after the madman only to discover that he was nowhere to be found. Maybe somebody tipped him off that Blessing was in the hospital or he just planned to kill her and disappear. The police got his picture and have declared him wanted.

After we put his picture out, another girl he put in the family way and tried to abort for also surfaced. She almost died. He ran away from where he was staying and moved to where our daughter encountered him.

Meanwhile, our daughter is struggling to get back to life. Tests have shown that her womb may be damaged and can only be rectified by medical procedures that are not available here in Ghana. I don't know what to do. I don't know how to raise that kind of money. And I can't watch my daughter die.

This whole mess has made me feel like a failed parent. How she has been dating a man without my knowledge baffles me. If she did not want to tell me, how could I have missed the signs? I am just a failure. Maybe things would have been different if you were here. You are very observant and have this intuition that could have saved the day.

The doctors at Korle Bu Teaching Hospital have assured me that she will live, but they say time is crucial if her womb is to be saved.

I am a sad woman here holding on to a thin hope and praying it does not snap. For now, the chances of coming to see you are slim. I need to be here for our daughter.

God willing, we shall see.

Bye for now

Your Okwy.

I was a wreck by the time I got to the last line. Alice was downcast too. I thanked her for coming and bid her farewell and Godspeed. She asked if I would not write any reply. I told her I would rather not. I declined to reply because I felt guilty: I brought all the mess upon myself and my family. I simply asked her to thank Okwy for me for all she was doing for our children.

I retired to my cell and tried to sleep, but that night sleep eluded me.

After Alice's visit, I stopped writing my wife. I did not try to find out how she was doing with the children. I knew that I could not be part of their world anymore, so they could go on living without me. Perhaps, this disconnection began the day I told my wife to do whatever she needed to satisfy her sexual urges; perhaps it began the day I decided to fund those activists. I decided that I would not be baggage for my family to drag along with them everywhere they went. I wanted them to live and live freely.

But one visiting day, Okwy came. I was shocked when I was told I had a visitor. I almost passed out when I saw Okwy.

My wife had lost some weight, but her beauty, which attracted me to her, was still very much intact. Her skin had lost some of its glow, but it still had the look of someone who had had a good life. I noticed a mark around her forehead but chose not to ask how or where she got it. She had been through a lot for me to trouble her about such flippant matter.

'I deliberately did not tell them my name because I have a feeling you may not want to see me,' she said as I hugged her after getting over the shock.

'It is good to see you again,' I said.

We sat down after the pleasantries and she fired the first salvo.

'Why didn't you write?'

I looked at her and emotion welled up in me.

'I did not know what to write. The information in your last letter overwhelmed me and I just could not think of what to say to you.'

From the look on her face, I guessed she had some good news.

'How is everything?' I asked.

'Things are looking up. Blessing has recovered and is back home and ready to look beyond the sad incident…'

'That is good,' I said.

41

There was this spark in her eyes that told me she had more to say.

'Do you remember Emeka Jibueze?' She asked.

Emeka was one of the contractors to the government when I was governor. His firm constructed all the flyovers we built during our time in office. He made billions doing contracts with our administration.

'I ran into him in Accra. He was very happy to see me and was willing to help. I did not think much of his promise until he came to see the children and me at home the day after I met him at the Accra Mall. He came with a cheque of five hundred thousand dollars and is arranging for our daughter to be taken abroad for proper treatments on her womb.'

'That is very kind of him,' I said.

But something told me she had more to say.

'My husband, please don't give up. Things can still be better,' she said.

I sensed that she was up to something and I asked: 'What are you driving at?'

'There is a prophet,' she began, but she stopped on seeing the expression on my face.

'Please, Okwy. Don't let some charlatan in a cassock take the money Emeka gave you. Take that money and start a new life,' I said sternly, my mood changing.

'It is not like that my dear,' she started to explain, but I wasn't interested.

She turned quiet when she saw my expression.

I thawed. 'What is it like?' I said, regarding her with pity for what she had to do, and anger over her gullibility.

'The prophet goes to the mountain in Iseyin, Oyo State regularly and I have been told if I go with him, he will pray, and a miracle will happen…'

'I hope you have not given this prophet any money,' I said.

Silence.

'Okwy, to the best of my knowledge, the only miracle that can happen is that I get to live. That means I will be allowed to grow old and die on my own. Anything outside that is wishful thinking. I beg you in God's name and in the name of everything you hold dear, whatever you have given for this miracle you are seeking, let it end there. Don't give more, please. I am happy you have enough money to expand your business and will be in a position to give Victor and Blessing the best. Do not let any smart cheat take advantage of your situation to make money he has not earned. These guys believe that we have some money stashed in some secret overseas accounts and will be quick to assist you. Okwy, you and I know we have no such money. There is nothing left. So take this lifeline Emeka is offering you and make good.'

She eventually confessed that the consultant to the prophet had already taken $5000 dollars from her.

'And that is enough,' I said, 'let it end there.'

I asked about the children.

'They are actually in Nigeria with my sister. Blessing is due for the U.S. for treatment soon; Emeka is perfecting the process. I did not feel it was right to bring them to come and see you. I am not sure I can handle the emotion the visit would generate.'

I understood her perfectly well.

'It is okay, dear. Please, forget this idea of going to any mountain in search of a miracle for me. I am happy Emeka remembered all we did for him. Please utilise the money well and I trust all will be well with you guys. As for me, just pray…'

'Don't complete that, honey. Please, don't.' Tears rolled down her cheeks as she said the words.

We remained silent for some minutes before time was up for her to leave.

'Thank you for coming and give my love to the children,' I said and stood. As she was about to leave, I decided to write a letter to Emeka. I pleaded with the warder to allow me some little time. He obliged.

Dear Emeka,

It is said that you only know those who are with you when you run into trouble. Okwy has told me everything you have done and are still doing for my family. Who would have thought that my insistence that you handle our bridge projects would turn into a lifeline for my family?

I thank you and I pray that you'll never find yourself in a tight corner like me. Please be straight in your dealings, and God will be with you. May the universe look kindly on you for your kindness.

Yours,

Nelson

After I wrote the letter, I stood and hugged my wife. I watched her go before I returned to my cell. As I walked back, I was glad that my family would be alright. It didn't matter what fate befell me now, or when. What mattered was that my progeny would live on, and tomorrow would be better for them. My life, I thought, would have ended well.

5

THIS THING CALLED LOVE

You resumed at Wells Petroleum Development Company's Warri office two months after you returned to Nigeria. The ambience was excellent. The office environment was great. The staff quarters were out of this world, and your colleagues were great. A car was practically waiting for you before you inked the acceptance letter. All these had absolutely nothing to do with your father, who by then had unfortunately vanished.

The circumstances of his disappearance, you assumed then, would haunt and hurt you for the rest of your life, no matter how you tried to put it behind you. It happened on the day you returned from the U.S. Mother told you he had chosen to come to the airport in Lagos to pick you up. He had flown into Lagos the day before and called her to tell her he got to Lagos in one piece. That was all you all knew. He never showed up at the airport.

Your mother almost lost it when after searching everywhere, including mortuaries, she came up with nothing. The police drew a blank. Days ran into weeks and weeks into months, and you all had no choice but to carry on with your lives. Resuming at Wells was a good distraction. And working in a conducive environment was healing.

It was years later that you found out that your worry over your father had been misplaced. Your sister discovered the truth. She had hinted at it in a letter before bringing Tobe and Helon to see you at the Underground Maximum Prison.

'My Dearest Sister,' Linda's letter had begun, *'I do not need to ask you how you are because I know you are not feeling fine. Your sons miss you so much and they talk about you every day. They find it difficult to believe you are capable of the offence for which you have been convicted and fervently pray that Jesus will open the eyes of the government and you will be set free.*

'Tobe says nice things about you every day. Helon sometimes wakes up in the middle of the night crying and praying for you, telling Jesus that you are the best mum in the world.'

The second part of the letter shook you to the bone marrow. It was about your father, who disappeared mysteriously in Lagos and you gave up as dead.

'I know you will be shocked by this. Our father is alive. He is old, but he is alive.'

You almost dropped the letter when you got to that part. But your hunger for the information made you go on. You were broken at the end of it. You had expected to read that your dad had been kidnapped and taken to some dungeon. It wasn't that you wanted something bizarre to have happened to your dad; you only hoped for an excuse good enough to justify his disappearance. But you were disappointed.

'I went to California for an event last week and saw a familiar face on a wheelchair. The man in the wheelchair looked like an eighty-year-old. I went closer and looked at him again and did not know when I shouted "Daddy!" He too looked at me and called out my name. I almost fell. I was excited. I was sad. I wanted answers.

'We retired to a restaurant to talk. What Daddy had to say broke my heart. In tears, he begged for my forgiveness. I wondered why. When he had done speaking, it all became clear. I hate to tell you this, but our father planned his disappearance. He became enamoured with his secretary, the fair-in-complexion one called Rose, and they eloped to the U.S. together. Daddy abandoned mum and us and started a new life with Rose. The girl ran away with all his money and credit cards and other valuables after living with him for five years and not having a child. His life crumbled, he became stranded, but shame made him stay back in the States, where I found him. He asked after you and Mum and I told him Mum was dead and you were in jail. He wanted to know why, so I told him the truth. That you were trying to help a man who had been robbed and dispossessed of his car on the highway and the man had died in your car before you made it to the hospital. I told him that the police had accosted you and called you a ritualist. You had been charged for murder and found guilty. He was still in tears when I left him at the restaurant and took a cab to my hotel. I have shed many tears. I could not sleep that night. How could Daddy have done this to us? To you? To me? To Mum? How?

'I am in shock, but as far as I am concerned, he is dead. He has been dead and will remain so. Don't think too much about him. He deserves everything Rose did to him. How coul d he abandon us because of another woman? It still baffles me. I told myself I would not go looking for him, even though he mentioned his address at a point in our discussion. He got what he deserved. We should let him sink in the hole he dug for himself.

'I will come to Nigeria soon with your children. They have been troubling me about seeing you and I have finally promised them. Expect us in the first week of October. I have already bought the tickets and got them confirmed. Once there is no cancellation of flight and such other unforeseen circumstances, we will be live and direct in Naija.

'Take good care of yourself and do not waste your time thinking about someone who did not think about us. Father is dead; let's have him buried.'

47

Your father's behaviour was a rude shock. He must have planned the whole thing for months and looked for an auspicious moment to realise it. Like your sister said, he was dead and he remained so to you.

All you looked forward to after putting your father in the grave was seeing your children. You counted the days till it finally came. They both jumped on you immediately you walked into the reception of the female wing of the prison. Linda joined them too. You all cried, laughed and talked. You prayed, too. It was like they should not go after staying one hour beyond the approved time.

As they left for their hotel, where they would tour some popular sights and see some family members before returning to the U.S., you wondered if you would ever see them again. Optimism took the better part of you. After all, no governor had signed death warrants in years. You reasoned that you would just be left in the prison till you aged and passed on. Or get a presidential pardon?

For reasons you could not fathom, the night of the day your kids came you found yourself thinking about your father, Magnus Akarue. As you sat on the bed, your mind wandered into the past, seeking out a good part of your once darling father who chose to shock you all.

You were his first child. You were born when he was 32 and your mother was 25. He had just returned to Nigeria from Oxford, where he bagged his first and second degrees when he married your mother, who was a teacher at the time.

Throughout your childhood, you had no cause to think that your father was unhappy with your mum. The two of them often wore matching clothes, attended events together and even ran a joint account which, in the real sense, was run by your mother and largely funded by your father.

Your father's relationship with your mother was so cordial that his family often joked she had fed him a love potion. It is by looking back now that you understand sarcasm and the nuances of adulthood, you are now not sure if those comments were playful. But you remember that your parents bore it well, and your father insisted on getting Mum's permission before giving out any money from what he chose to call 'the commonwealth.'

Most of your father's property bore your mother's name. Even when she encouraged him to buy some property in his name, he would flare up and insisted that he had things just how he wanted it. He ensured that your mother had the best things in life. Her vacations were spent in the best of destinations: Hawaii. Singapore. The Bahamas. Paris. All the exotic places she could think of.

Your father appeared to not decide without seeking your mother's consent. The choices of schools that you and your sister went to were subject to your mother's approval. He always said that your mother's instinct was infallible. So, he left weighty decisions about you and your sister to her judgement.

On one occasion, your father needed to reclaim his property in the village. The building housed his mother while she was alive but was taken over by his sister after the old woman died. He sent your mother to do the assignment. She turned it down, and he had to lie to his sister that he took a loan from the bank and the bank was after his property, so, she had to vacate. She did, grudgingly. When she eventually found out your father lied, she placed the blame on your mother.

Another incident that would forever make it difficult for you to understand the reason your father ran away with Rose happened when you were twelve. Your driver at the time, Lukman, disappeared with your father's 550 dollars the day he returned from a trip to

Norway. Your dad was furious and threatened to arrest his guarantor when Lukman could not be found. He was livid. But your mum did not think he should arrest the guarantor. Your father agreed in seconds and stopped boiling with anger. He even smiled and joked. Such was your mother's influence on him, which you believed could only have been because he loved her. So, you now wondered, at what point did he stop loving her? At what point did he become unhappy?

He was a doting father who really devoted all to his children. There were times he insisted on driving you to school himself. He visited you more than your mother while you were abroad studying, and he never came empty-handed. He knew what each of his children liked and the idea of what gift to buy was never a problem. He was a great father and husband in every sense of the word.

So, when did the love die? You found yourself asking. Did Rose use a charm on him? You could not but ask this question because there seemed to be no grounds for your father's actions. You did not believe in the efficacy of juju, but as you considered your father's actions, you told yourself that it had to be something stronger than natural. You wished you could see him and ask some questions. That night, when your exhausted body could not sleep, your emotions oscillated between pity for the father on a wheelchair, and anger for the father who left the familiarity and security of your home for the novelty of a strange woman's thighs. Eventually, the anger won.

Despite your anger, you were grateful to know what happened. The knowledge brought closure to you and took away your guilt about his disappearance. You had consistently beaten yourself up that you were the one who made him disappear. If only he had not come to Lagos to welcome you. If maybe, you had not announced your coming and decided to give them a surprise instead. If only... Now, you knew.

You were also happy that your mother was not alive to hear the news. It would have broken her in many ways than your mind could conceive; in many painful ways that you would not be able to watch.

During that sleepless night, you remembered what happened when you touched down in Lagos. You had not been told that your father was coming to fetch you. So when you did not see anyone at the airport, you were only slightly worried. So, you went ahead with your own plan of spending the night in Lagos with Precious, a friend you met in the U.S.

You and Precious Okonkwo became friends in your first year at the university and did a lot of things together. She grew up in Lagos, where her father was a big shot who sat on the board of some blue-chip companies.

Lagos was lively as ever. Commerce thrived on every available space and you noted that the city seemed to have a music of its own to which it moved in rhythm. The weather was beautiful and it was not the rainy season which was just as well because the roads would be terrible in the rain. You were able to adapt to the weather not just because it was summer in Washington; you adapted because it was Nigeria, and it was home.

What you saw that night made you remember a story you once heard about a father who was sleeping with his daughter. The story had seemed a tall tale until you saw Precious and her father. That night, they kissed and did everything typical lovers would do. They obviously thought you were sound asleep. You were until the sound of their making out woke you. When you acted as if you were moving in your sleep, her father broke off the kiss and whispered, 'Be gentle Precious, don't wake your friend.' After that, father and daughter kissed their way out of the room.

Your stomach churned. Precious's mother had died. You

wondered if the incest started after she died or before. Perhaps, you thought, it was the knowledge of the alliance between father and daughter that sent her to an early grave.

The next morning, at first light, you sneaked out of their house without saying goodbye. You blacked them out of your life after that night.

So you pondered now knowing your father was alive. Alive and on a wheelchair. Looking older as your sister had described, but alive nonetheless. You did not cause his death. He disappeared. You were blameless in his case and innocent for another man's death too.

You now knew this. You felt lighter. Less burdened. You felt innocent of all crimes perceived and supposedly factual. You had to prove your innocence. You wouldn't die for a crime you did not commit. A death you did not cause. You believed you had the right to fight for Tobe and Helon. To be there for them.

Weeks passed and you were still incarcerated, none of the lawyers you had been allowed to contact would represent you and have your case reopened. It was an open and shut case, they said. "Why was the man in your car?" one asked, even after you had explained why he was there.

You were about to give up again when Precious Okonkwo walked into the prison one day. You stared at her in shock; she hadn't changed. She gasped and shouted your name.

"Jacinta, what are you doing here?" You got up and walked over to her. She hugged you as soon as you were close enough. "What are you doing here?" She asked again. You burst into tears.

She called to the security guards and requested you be given some time in the waiting room, they obliged. When you were finally seated, you poured out your heart, telling her about how you got into prison, about your father who was not dead and about you wanting to engage the system if you could to prove your innocence.

Precious was quiet for a few minutes. "Jacinta, remember what you saw the night we returned from the U.S. between my father and me?" You could only nod. "Well, I knew you had seen us when you were nowhere to be found the next morning. What I did not know was if our secret would become the talk of the town with you mentioning it to someone who would speak to someone else until it became news for the tabloids. So for a long time, my father and I expected the worst until it seemed as if you had disappeared. It is now my turn to repay you for your silence." Again you just nodded.

You later discovered Precious was a top lawyer and had come to the prison that day to see a new client. She had your case reopened. Accusing the system of jungle justice. No autopsy of the man's corpse had been carried out. No investigation into your background had been done. No establishment for a motive as to why you would be a ritualist was confirmed. She went on and on, and after four court appearances, your case was struck out on circumstantial evidence.

You collapsed that day after the ruling by the judge. It seemed surreal that you would walk out free from the prison's gates after the years you had spent waiting to be hung. You looked to your father and sister who were in court. You smiled, he smiled, Linda smiled. You could not understand this thing called love. But you understood second chances.

6

BETTER THAN THE DEVIL

No one told me his offence, and I did not ask.

I simply obeyed orders and killed him. He was one of the three Ile-Ife indigenes who died at my hands. I later found out he was dating a girl the second-in-command of our confraternity was interested in. The girl had refused 2iC's advances because she already had a boyfriend. Our frat sniffed out the boyfriend, and I was asked to take him out. All for the good of the confraternity!

I never carried out any jobs except the ones ordered by the Cappo. Since I was out obeying orders, I told myself that God would not count the sins as mine. That way, I was able to push the guilt aside and do my job with finesse.

By the time I was graduating and heading to the Law School in Lagos, I had deleted sixteen students, two lecturers, one security guard and three Ile-Ife indigenes who tried to double-cross the confraternity.

I lost count of the number of girls I checked their pride. I was even part of a crew that jointly humbled two lecturers with big buttocks and succulent breasts. One of them had breasts so big that her husband should not bother using a pillow. Yes, I am talking about rape, but we were simply told to check the girls' pride. I can still recollect how I enjoyed squeezing those lecturers' boobs. Nothing personal, I was obeying orders and pleasing my instincts in the process.

I was sober in Law School and almost came top of my set. But a day after I finished my bar exams in 1981, I received a visitor in my hostel. I had packed my bags and was ready to return to my mother in Port Harcourt when our last Cappo showed up in my room. On Campus, Cappo was not an average student. He was not bright. His tests and assignments were done for him; nobody knew how he wrote his examinations. Nobody spoke about such things.

Cappo was the son of a quick-fingered civil servant who was so witty at stealing government money that he was referred to in some quarters as 'Finger of God or FG' for short. It was said that other civil servants apprenticed themselves to him to learn how to steal. But, nobody had any proof; he too had nothing to show for it, except being a chronic womaniser.

When Cappo showed up at my door that afternoon, we hugged like two lost friends.

'Cappo,' I said after we settled down. 'It's so good to see you.'

'Cappo?' He responded dismissively. 'Please leave that small boy stuff for university people, abeg. We are men now. It's Mr Obioma Johnson, please.'

I laughed. He didn't; he was serious.

'Alright, Mr Johnson,' I said. 'It has a nice ring to it too.'

'Thank you,' he said and we burst into laughter.

'Thanks, man. I appreciate all those stuff you helped me take care of on the campus. I appreciate you, brother.' Johnson said, hugging my huge frame once more.

'Don't mention, my brother,' I said.

'Don't say that. You did well for me. All those times I would be in Lagos chasing money, you were running those errands, man. You are a dependable person,' he said.

'And all that money you were hustling for in Lagos sustained me,' I replied. 'You were generous.'

'You deserved all that money, brother. You did well.' Johnson said, surveying my poky room.

At that point, I was beginning to wonder why he showed up at my hostel, just a day before I left the premises. I had been secretly grateful to God that I had left the campus unscathed. I was never caught, so my position as a lawyer was still safe.

'We need your service,' he said.

I was taken aback. 'What? Cappo…'

'Mr Obioma Johnson,' he said.

'Mr Obio…' I stood. 'Who is we?'

'A band of brothers; you're one of us.'

'One of you? Cappo, I thought that stuff ended on campus.'

'Yes, the small boy stuff ended on campus. Out here in the real world, we are into the real stuff. We do stuff that have real consequences. We are the movers and shakers of this country. And you,' he stood and tapped me on the shoulder, 'must now take your place among the brothers.'

'But, Cappo, I am a lawyer, a…'

'Yes, you are. And there are many like you among our ranks. Big men, SANs and other people. We are a league of professionals. And, perhaps, you now understand why you can no longer say Cappo. It's Mr Obioma Johnson. Listen, I don't have to break this down to you; you are one of us. Take your place.' His visage had become stern.

At that instant, I regretted the day I agreed to join the fraternity. But I also recalled that I wasn't left with much choice. It was either I joined them, left the campus, got killed or maimed. I remember that I had been told that they wanted me, and that was that.

Obioma Johnson meant business, and my protests meant nothing to him. He spoke on as if I had not objected.

'Take this key. I have reserved a room for you at Aces Suites on Adeniyi Adesina Way, off Kingsway Road. I will meet you there at midnight to give you further instructions and information,' Johnson said and made for the door.

Just when I thought he had left, the door creaked open again. He said softly, 'Barrister, please don't trade your mother's life for stupidity.'

The expression on his face did not match his tone of voice. It was one of those expressions that spoke volumes. And I knew of the possibilities in that expression.

My room at Aces Suites was a paradise. The bed was gold-plated, the rug glittered with opulence, and the fittings were breath-taking.

I lay on the bed and wondered how Johnson was able to afford to lodge me in such a hotel. We finished school together. He studied Architecture and had not even done the mandatory one-year national service. So, he could not have landed a big job that could make money answer his summons.

Amid this beauty, I felt like I was about to swallow the udala seed not minding the size of my throat.

I turned on the television. The Nigerian Television Authority, which we fondly called NTA, was again airing a broadcast of President Shehu Shagari. Since the National Party of Nigeria (NPN) candidate had been sworn in on October 1, 1979, to govern, President Shagari had become a regular face on our screens. When the former teacher sneezed, the station caught a cold.

Shagari ran a government of 61 ministers, 24 of whom were of cabinet rank. The others were without portfolios. He was accused of giving more slots to Muslims than Christians. He also came under fire for making extensive use of the Cabinet Office, made up of senior professional civil servants, to the detriment of political appointees as typical in a presidential system.

These were some of the issues he was addressing on NTA at the time I turned on the television. He faulted the claims that he did not have total control of his cabinet.

'Fairness, justice and, above all, the fear of God Almighty have guided every single decision taken by this government. No part should feel cheated. We have been fair and we will remain so,' the president explained, with the interviewer nodding his head in agreement.

It did not occur to me that the reason I was in the hotel had anything to do with the politics of the 1983 presidential election, which turned out to be the worst election in Nigeria's history. I was being asked to spearhead the violence, arson, vote-rigging and other malpractices that defined that era and gave the military the excuse to usurp power.

A fall in the price of oil forced Shagari, two days after assuming office for a second term, to announce an austerity programme. Generals Muhammadu Buhari and Tunde Idiagbon seized the momentum and removed what one of them described as the 'inept and corrupt administration that left Nigeria a beggar nation.'

I was still soaking in Shagari's explanations on NTA when there was a knock at the door. I immediately assumed it must be Johnson. He was here to kill my curiosity. But it was not Johnson. It was the manager of the hotel, whom I had met shortly before being checked in.

I opened the door, and he handed me an envelope. He said it was from Johnson. I shut the door after him and made for the couch to open the envelope. The content almost took my life—crisp twenty Naira notes. I counted. N2000. This was 1981; it was more than I had ever owned. More cash to come later, the letter in the envelope read.

I was still in shock when there was another knock at the door. This time I silently prayed it would be Johnson. But my prayer was not answered. It was a waiter from the room service unit. He told me he had been told to serve me a befitting meal. He looked at me as if I was royalty or a VIP. I let him in, and he placed the stainless steel silverware he was carrying on the centre table. He told me to please call the switchboard if I needed anything else.

After he left, I opened the dish and saw a whole grilled chicken, a platter of fried rice and a bottle of champagne. The ensemble was completed with a set of cutlery, one tumbler and a champagne flute. And there was another envelope. I opened it, and there was a note addressed to me: 'Please enjoy yourself, Mr Michael Ekiwetan Esq. Signed: Management.'

I could touch neither the drink, the chicken, nor taste of the fried rice. I was full, full of expectation. I needed to know what I was up against.

At a point, I remembered that Johnson said he was going to come by midnight. I looked at the time; it was 8:33pm. I had about three hours, thirty minutes to wait. Curiosity would surely kill me.

I decided to eat some chicken and wash it down with the champagne. Forty-five minutes later, I had gulped down about half the bottle and eaten almost all of the chicken, the fried rice remained untouched. I started feeling tipsy. I checked the alcoholic content of the champagne. Eighteen whole per cent!

I did not know when I fell asleep. A knock at the door woke me. I checked the time; it was midnight. The television was still on, but the station had closed, and it was just the blank screen and static.

This time, it was Johnson.

'Ekiwetan,' he said as he strode in.

'Johnson, what is this all about?' I asked. 'Do you want me to take out the president? Or, why so much money? And…'

'Yes, I want you to take some people out, but the president isn't one of them.'

'I am done with that life, Johnson. I told you. I am not doing this stuff.'

Johnson smiled. 'I'll let you know when you are done. Your target is Alhaji Sanni Ojo. He, his wife, his children and everybody in his house must be taken out before daybreak.'

I made to object, but he continued: 'His mansion is on Abimbola Kesington Way, off Adeniran Ogunsanya. I am sure you know where that is. Once you get on that street, you will see the house. It is the biggest and the only white house there. The foolish man even inscribes "Sanni Ojo White House" on it. So, it is easy for you to locate.'

He started fiddling with a suitcase. I hadn't noticed that he came into the room with any suitcase. He brought out three bottles with some liquid content.

'This is all you need to do a clean job. You don't need a gun or anything. You don't even need to confront anyone. Once you get there, just throw these into the compound and disappear. But make sure you throw one at the generator house. We have received intel that he keeps kegs and kegs of fuel in that place. A car is waiting outside to take you. Don't disappoint us. If you do, you will be gambling with your mother's life. But if you do a neat job, there is more where that envelope came from. You can even set up a practice.'

I thought briefly about the whole scenario and felt relaxed with the fact that I did not have to use a gun or machete.

'But what is the content of this bottle?' I asked.

'What you have in your hands is a petrol bomb spiked with orisirisi. Just throw it, and the house will catch fire and subsequently kill the occupants. But make sure you throw at least one into the generator house. It's hard to miss.'

Before I could ask any more questions, he headed for the door and turned to say: 'When you return from the assignment, the manager will give you another envelope. I know how to get you if you mess up. I'll be seeing you.'

A few minutes later, the intercom buzzed. It startled me as if I was not aware of the facility's existence. I did not feel like answering it. But when it would not stop ringing, I grabbed it and said a very weak 'hello'.

There was silence from the other end — a dead silence. I said hello four more times. Still, it was a graveyard silence. But just when I was about to drop the handset, I heard something that sounded like a 'hello'.

'Hello, hello,' I cooed.

But there was no answer from the other end. Perhaps my ears were playing pranks on me. I put down the receiver with a mixture of fear and anger threatening to seethe my inside.

A thought was about taking shape in my heart when the intercom came alive again. *Graun! Graun! Graun!* I felt like smashing it. But in no time I was clutching the handset.

'Hello…'

'Hi Michael,' said the voice from the other end.

'What is it?' I asked.

'Nothing much, nothing much…'

I soon recognised the voice as Johnson's. Why was he calling me on the intercom?

And then, dead silence.

'Please say what you want to say,' I begged.

'Nothing. But I am watching you. The mission must not be fucked up!'

He hung up. As I dropped the receiver, I needed no pastor, imam or babalawo to tell me I had to answer the devil's call.

Obioma Johnson's words, 'Don't trade your mother's life for stupidity,' kept ringing in my head minutes after he left. At 2am, I stepped outside, to the lobby and to the compound. A floodlight flashed at me twice as I stepped out. I went to the car and met a stern-looking young man who told me he was the driver assigned to me. He took me to Abimbola Kesington Way, but not to the house. He said he was asked to drop me and wait for my return. I walked to the street, located the beautiful house and threw the bottles as I was instructed. Balls of fire rose as the bottles hit the targets. I ran to the car.

The next morning, I returned to Port Harcourt. I got to Port Harcourt in the evening since I travelled by road. My mother was very happy to receive me. While my mother and I were rejoicing over my return, a neighbour asked my mother to come and see wonder on television. I followed the two of them and right there on television was the evil I wrought in Lagos before rushing back to Port Harcourt.

The news had it that Alhaji Ojo, his two wives and eight of their children and domestic hands burnt to death in a house fire. The police said they were investigating the cause of the fire, which neighbours said started with a big bang. Alhaji Ojo, revealed the news, was a financier of a political party.

That night I could not sleep. I had N4,000 crisp notes in my kitty, but I was far from happy. I caused the death of eleven people in one fell swoop. Perhaps, Satan would not do worse to one family.

These days, as I look around my chambers, the one I started with the money I received from Johnson, I wonder if my work as a civil defence and human rights lawyer is enough. I wonder if Obioma Johnson, now a special adviser to the president on infrastructure, is watching me, bidding his time to send me on another job.

7

OTAPIAPIA

It was her first holiday since she resumed at the Federal University of Agriculture, Abeokuta. Technically, it wasn't a holiday; it was a strike. Her first since she became an undergraduate. Idera was excited to be in Lagos again, but she was not prepared for what she saw on entering the new two-bedroom apartment into which Aunty Rebecca and her husband had moved. She knocked on the door and waited a few seconds before she turned the knob. The door creaked open only for her to behold a man and a woman scrambling to cover their nakedness. The woman was her precious Aunty Rebecca, her breasts jiggling like a bell. The man was not Uncle Solagbade, Aunty Rebecca's husband; it was a man who Idera knew way back as a molue driver.

'How are you, darling?' Aunty Rebecca said, the molue driver hiding behind her, struggling to wear his trousers.

'Fine ma,' Idera said, looking at the floor where her bag had fallen.

'Go in and freshen up,' Aunty Rebecca said, with neither shame nor remorse in her voice.

As she made to leave, she noticed a wad of naira notes on the chair, not far from the molue driver who looked like he was dying of shame. There were at least two used condoms, and she knew that the action did not just begin. Aunty Rebecca followed her immediately she entered the room.

'You must tell no one what you have just seen. You are a woman, and I am sure you will understand with time that when a woman's needs are not met, she must find a way around it. My husband is never at home; he has no time for me. He thinks money is all I need, but I need more than that. I need him to be here. I have heard of him; he has women in almost every town that he passes. I have heard from reliable sources that he has a woman each in Ore and Eiyenkorin, another in Mokwa, another in Jebba and another in Sabongari in Kano. But he expects me to be here waiting for him. You are my blood and must take sides with me. With your mother dead, and your father dead-alive, I am the only one you have. Do you hear me?'

'Yes ma,' Idera said, entering a bloodless oath of secrecy with the woman who had told her to trust no one but God. Now, it made sense; it would never have occurred to her that Aunty Rebecca could cheat on her husband and right in their home, a new home for which the same man paid, to better their lot.

'He leaves me here for months. No wonder I have not been able to have a child all these years. I am a woman; I have blood flowing in my veins. I have needs. I will not resign to fate. I will take care of myself and that is all I have done. I have not killed anybody; I have only kept myself alive,' she said, reaching for the hand of her niece.

Peace eluded Idera when, the day after, Aunty Rebecca's husband returned after one month of being away. He held his wife with a rare affection and that broke Idera's heart. She was imprisoned by silence and guilt that washed over her. She felt the man deserved to know but remembered Aunty Rebecca's words that the man had other women in towns along his path to the North. Then she felt she was right to have cheated on him too. *Do me I do you God no go vex*, she thought to herself.

Aunty Rebecca knew how to act. She showered her husband with affection so much that Idera became disgusted. Her mother, God rest her soul, had told her that cheating was evil and anyone involved was the devil's apprentice.

Before Idera went to bed, Uncle Solagbade summoned her to the sitting room and fear enveloped her; she wondered if the man had heard some rumours and wanted to confirm from her.

'How is school?' Uncle Solagbade asked, adjusting the wrapper tied from his waist down.

'Fine sir,' she stuttered.

'Hope all is well.'

'Yes sir.'

'So, you people are on strike again?'

'Yes, sir. I am praying it won't last long.'

'I hope so too.'

'Thank you, sir.'

'I am happy you have put your mother's death and your father's disappointment behind you. God will be with you. Just continue to be a good girl; your aunt and I will do everything we can for you. Idera, you are our daughter now. Do you understand?'

'Yes. Thank you, sir.'

Relief washed over Idera when Uncle Solagbade said that was all he wanted to say. Her aunt was by his side while he talked to her. Aunty Rebecca glanced as Idera gave her a barely perceptible raise of her eyebrow.

That night, for the first time since she started staying with them, Idera was tempted to tiptoe to the couple's bedroom door to listen for signs of intimacy. She wanted to see how a woman could show affection to two different men a day apart. But she resisted the temptation and went to sleep.

As usual, Uncle Solagbade left after two days and the molue driver returned, sleeping with Aunty Rebecca on her husband's bed every other day. Aunty Rebecca must have given him the confidence that Idera would never tell, so he carried on as if he was in his own home. He even started buying Idera gifts and encouraging her to ask him for anything she wanted. In Idera's presence, he would grab her aunt's buttocks and breasts and tickle her, and the woman would giggle like an eighteen-year-old shocked by a sudden wetness between her thighs. Then, one day, he came when Aunty Rebecca had gone to the market.

'Good afternoon sir,' Idera greeted him.

'Good afternoon Idera. Where is your aunt?'

'In the market, sir. She said you should wait; that she would soon return.'

He waited. Ten minutes later, he asked Idera to come and sit beside him. He was wearing brown chinos trousers on an Adire top. His beer belly made him look like one of those men Idera and her friends on campus called improper fraction. As Idera moved closer and he opened his mouth, she nearly fainted; the smell of alcohol oozed out with a potency she had never perceived before. She moved back and he asked what the problem was.

'Nothing,' she replied.

'I want to take care of you,' he said.

'Thank you, sir.'

Then he made to touch her breasts. Idera moved back right on time to prevent his hand from doing his will. This man must be mad, she told herself. She remembered what she had learnt in her secondary school about warding off unwanted advances from the opposite sex. She walked away to show that she was not interested. Suddenly, the molue driver grabbed her from behind. She did not know where the energy came from, but she turned quickly and dealt the man a heavy blow in the face.

'Ye!' he screamed.

He was still holding his face when Aunty Rebecca came in, bearing a black polythene bag with vegetables and other ingredients. She dropped the nylon and asked what was going on.

'This man,' Idera pointed, 'is a he-goat,' she said, anger threatening to choke her. 'He was trying to touch my breasts, and he grabbed my bum-bum.'

'What!' Aunty Rebecca screamed and launched at the molue driver. 'Useless man, so you want to be doing me and doing my daughter. I give you my food, I give you my body and you'll sometimes take my money and yet you cannot keep your hands off my child. You unfortunate mad man. Oya, get out of my house!'

Idera was glad her aunt believed her. She remembered reading a book about a housegirl whose madam caught with her husband and still blamed the girl for seducing her husband. The man was still holding his face when Aunty Rebecca pushed him out of the door and told him never to come back.

'I am sorry,' Aunty Rebecca said after shutting the door. 'I didn't know he was that kind of person. The he-goat. Thank God you were bold enough to deal with him. Some other girls would have been afraid or even wanted his money.'

Aunty Rebecca brooded for weeks. There were times she would pace the sitting room and talk to herself. Idera wondered how Aunty

Rebecca could feel betrayed by a man who she betrayed her husband to please. Idera was pleased by the turn of events, thinking that her aunt would stick to her husband. But it was not the case; a tailor soon took the place of the molue driver.

The tailor was a gentleman. He never tried to touch Idera. In fact, he shied away from talking to her and faced the only business he had in the apartment. He was not brash and impulsive like the molue driver, and he kept his trysts with Aunty Rebecca in the bedroom. He visited only when he was sure Aunty Rebecca was around. And Idera was beginning to take a liking to him when her aunt returned one day from the market with a swollen face.

'Did you fall in a gutter?' Idera asked her aunt, worry written all over her. 'Should I help you to put water on the fire so that I can mop your swollen face? Do you need anything?'

She asked the questions many times but her aunt, who was writhing in pain, would not answer. She simply took a pain reliever and was about to retire to bed when Idera asked her again about what happened and Aunty Rebecca met her with a frozen gaze. 'Stop pestering me,' she said icily. Idera nodded and went to her room, angry and almost in tears.

Idera found out the truth the next day. She ran into a girl, Busola, her classmate in primary school. Busola told Idera that she saw her aunt and the tailor's wife fighting in the market. The tailor's wife, according to Busola, kept calling Aunty Rebecca a thief but never bothered to say what she stole. But Idera could piece together the details, which she kept to herself. She did not even share Busola's revelation with her aunt. The tailor never came to their flat again.

A week after the incident with the tailor's wife, Aunty Rebecca fell ill. She did not go to the hospital; she took herbs. She claimed it would heal her in no time. After a week, when the malaria and typhoid herbs had not manifested their healing powers, Aunty Rebecca did not relent. She sent Idera to the market to get new concoctions. Uncle Solagbade came back home the next weekend.

Uncle Solagbade asked his wife to go to the hospital.

'There is no need,' she said, re-tying her Ankara wrapper to her chest. 'The herbs are working. I am feeling better.'

'You are not serious,' Uncle Solagbade said. 'I'm taking you to the hospital myself.'

Idera followed them to the hospital in a taxi. There was a large crowd at the General Hospital when they got there. They got a tally number, which showed there were 101 patients before Aunty Rebecca. After four hours of waiting, it was Aunty Rebecca's turn. Idera stayed outside while husband and wife went in to see the doctor.

After a while, they both came out of the consulting room with a paper and headed for the lab. Idera knew that her aunt was going there to get tested. Was her aunt pregnant? She wondered. The tests were done and the doctor admitted Aunty Rebecca for observation. She would be released when the results of the tests came and they knew exactly what they were dealing with.

Idera went home quickly to bring a few things that her aunt needed and returned to stay with her in the hospital. She remembered the doctor's name, Dr Olugbile, because she saw it on her aunt's card. The results of the tests came out in three days and all hell was let loose.

Dr Olugbile came into the hospital room and asked to see Uncle Solagbade alone. But Aunty Rebecca insisted that he say whatever he had to say in front of her family. After all, she said, she was the one concerned. When the doctor glanced at Idera, Aunty Rebecca said it was okay.

'Alright, then,' the doctor said. 'The tests we conducted show that all your symptoms have nothing to do with a pregnancy. However, we found something. Madam, I am afraid, you tested positive to HIV.'

'What?' Uncle Solagbade shouted. Aunty Rebecca burst into tears. Idera was silent; she did not know what to do.

The doctor continued speaking. 'Sir, I'll need to run a test on you to find out if you are infected. Please know that HIV is not a death sentence. It is just a condition and it can be managed. If you eat right and take your drugs, you will be able to keep your viral load low, and still live a normal life. Please take heart.'

Aunty Rebecca was still in tears when the doctor asked Uncle Solagbade to please come with him for a test. Idera stayed with her aunt to prevent her from doing anything to herself. While her aunt sobbed, Idera wondered who among her aunt's men gave her the virus. Was it the brash Molue driver or the quiet fashion designer?

Uncle Solagbade's result came back negative. And that was when he lost his silence. Where had she gotten the virus? She hadn't gotten it from him. So, this was what she had been doing while he was travelling all over the nation, making a living for both of them? Uncle Solagbade did not shout, but his voice, though low, was hard and accusing.

'Ehen? Useless man,' Aunty Rebecca started. 'So you have found your voice because you got lucky? You think I haven't heard about you? All those women in all the towns you frequent. You think I don't know about Hadiza in Tundun-Wada, or all those women in Ore, Eiyenkorin and Kano? And the motor park girls? So, because you got lucky, you want to start talking to me anyhow? Who pushed me into this mess in the first place? What did you expect? That you would leave me at home for weeks and come back tired, used and I would be waiting for you? Unfortunate man.'

Idera's aunt rendered this tirade in tears. She was one of those people who cried when they were angry.

Somehow, it seemed as though they had both forgotten that Idera was there. And Idera witnessed it all, her aunt's silent hysteria and the guilt that seemed to descend on Uncle Solagbade like a cloak, especially when Aunty Rebecca mentioned Hadiza in Tundun-Wada. He was guilty, Idera saw from his facial expression; she probably would never know how much. It looked to Idera as if Uncle Solagbade would thaw and ask for his wife's forgiveness, but he hardened up again and stormed out of the hospital room.

The doctor refused to discharge Aunty Rebecca before she saw a counsellor. Meanwhile, her health had improved and the rashes had cleared. Idera refused to leave her aunt's side. Uncle Solagbade returned, sober, and promising to take care of her. Aunty Rebecca had turned to the wall when he said he was sorry to have spoken the way he did. Once Aunty Rebecca was strong enough, the doctor invited her, her husband and Idera to the counsellor's office.

'I am sorry to hear about your diagnosis,' the counsellor began. Her voice was mellow and soothing. It was the kind of voice that told you that you could confide in its owner. It was a confident voice, assured of everything that it gave volume. It was also a practised voice – perhaps, Idera thought, she had said the words she was about to say to many people before. Idera wondered if the counsellor would mock her aunt when they all left, or if her case would become the subject of talk at the counsellor's dinner table.

'HIV is not a death sentence. In fact, you can still live a normal life. All you need to do is to exercise regularly, take your ARVs and have regular checkups. That way, your health can be managed and you will live a long, fulfilling life. HIV does not kill; it is when it explodes into full-blown AIDS that death is imminent. But that doesn't have to happen.'

'And sir,' the counsellor turned to Uncle Solagbade, 'you can still have sexual relations with your wife. Just make sure you use a condom every time.'

'My life is over, Doctor,' Aunty Rebecca said, in tears.

'My dear wife,' Uncle Solagbade said, 'all will be well.'

'You liar! All will be well. Will all be well when you leave me and go on your long trips to be with other women? Will all be…'

'Calm down, Madam,' the counsellor said. Aunty Rebecca calmed. 'Most people do not know, but there are other diseases that kill more and faster than HIV. It is the fear of HIV that actually kills, not the virus. Please take your meds and come for regular check-up. You will be fine.'

'Thank you, Doctor,' Aunty Rebecca responded.

'Sir,' the counsellor turned to Uncle Solagbade, 'and my girl,' she indicated Idera, 'please take care of her. You can't catch HIV by caring for her, using the same toilet, touching her or even eating from the same plate. But make sure you avoid sharing sharp objects and other things. All of you will be alright.'

'Thanks, Ma'am,' Idera said. Uncle Sologbade nodded.

That day, after a last check-up, Idera and her aunt returned home. At home, Idera moved around quietly preparing food and doing what she could to make her aunt comfortable.

Three weeks had passed since Aunty Rebecca returned from the hospital. She continued to brood and cry at every opportunity. Uncle Solagbade, after staying a week, returned to his job, but not before promising to be home as soon as possible. He pleaded with Idera to look after her aunt and she promised she would.

One evening, Aunty Rebecca suddenly got up, brightening like the sun breaking from gloomy clouds and said she was done crying. She asked Idera to please get her two bottles of liquid insecticide to get rid of the mosquitoes in her room. Idera was happy to see her aunt worrying about something other than her health status, so she hurried. She offered her aunt food, and Aunty Rebecca ate lots of it. That night, as they prepared to sleep, the news came on that ASUU and the federal government had reached an agreement; therefore, the strike had been called off. Idera was happy and her aunt rejoiced with her. Eventually, they went to sleep.

That night, Idera felt a deathly silence around the house. But she put it down to the fact that she was awake. Night times were supposed to be silent, she reasoned. It was probably because she was thinking about school – now that the strike had ended.

The next morning, Idera went to her aunt's room and found her still sleeping. She almost turned back but decided to wake her up. It was then that she saw that her aunt was lying rather still. When she reached out to touch her, there was no warmth. Idera's eyes fell on the two bottles of insecticide on the table, under which there was a note. Idera raised her aunt's hand and dropped it, and it fell, limp. Idera shouted for help; at the same time she opened the note. It read simply,

I drank the otapiapia. I can't live with AIDS.
Take care of yourself.

8

WHEN TRUTH DIES

I step out of my Oaks Apartment flat and the harsh Houston sun almost blinds me. I rub my hand over my eyes. My vision becomes clearer and I see an apparition. Driving a 2019 Corolla towards the exit gate is my husband. Yes, my husband, the one who died three months ago.

I clear my face again and he is still there; he is not a ghost. Back home in Nigeria, people would have thrown sand at him to confirm that he is not a ghost.

In my dazed state, he drives out of the exit gate. I open the door and return to the sitting room. The groceries at Sam's Club can wait.

'Are you back?' My son says in his Texan accent.

I walk to my room without answering his question. I sit on the bed and ruminate over what I just saw. I must be hallucinating, I said to myself.

He died, yes, and we buried him. We took him home to Abeokuta. I have his death certificate. I saw his corpse lowered into the grave. I poured dust on his coffin, and I watched as the grave was filled up. I returned to the graveside to lay flowers and shed tears.

I remember how he died. My Omoniyi died in the bathroom.

We were together in the room when he excused himself to use the convenience. Ten minutes later, he was still there. Thirty minutes he was not yet out. I called his name and there was no answer. I called again and there was still no response. I stood and rushed in and there he was in the bathtub, his eyes half closed. I screamed and tried to lift him. I felt for his pulse but there was nothing.

We were alone. The children were in school. Both of us were off work that day and had planned to spend it together.

I grabbed my phone and dialed 911. They told me an ambulance was coming and that I should keep my husband warm and elevated.

The paramedics soon arrived, affixed an oxygen mask to my husband and rushed him to the hospital. I cried all through the trip. I prayed too. I was not allowed to go beyond the reception of the Intensive Care Unit.

Minutes later, I was invited to see the doctor.

'I am sorry ma'am,' the doctor said. 'Your husband was brought in dead.'

Somehow, I knew that my husband had died before we got to the hospital, but I was hanging on to some glimmer of hope that they could do something, just anything to bring him back. That glimmer had been dashed against the headboard of an expert's confirmation.

The minutes after that, until I left the hospital, remain a blur to me.

These days, everywhere I turn, I see him. I am not myself and cry a lot; my children are confused and cry too, especially when I'm crying, so we sit together bonded in our tears. And just when I begin to get over it, I see him again. This time, not a semblance. But my husband, in the flesh, and he is talking with a neighbour. I shout his name. He doesn't look back. I shout some more but he doesn't flinch.

I run towards them and continue shouting. When I hold him and call his name, he is surprised, but he says softly 'I am not Omoniyi.' It is his voice. I pass out.

When I regain consciousness at the hospital in Bessonet, Ismael, my Indian neighbour, and my children are around me.

'Good to have you back,' Ismael says.

I look around to see if my husband, the one who claims not to be my husband, is anywhere around.

'He is my husband,' I say to Ismael with tears rolling down my cheeks.

'Who?' Ismael asks, looking confused.

'The man who was with you.'

Ismael never met Omoniyi, my husband. We moved into Oaks Apartment a month after he passed. I could not cope with living in that apartment on Big Thicket Drive, where we shared beautiful memories.

'He is not your husband. He is my friend. He just moved to Houston from Lagos. I knew him right from Ilupeju where I was born.'

His statement confuses me. My husband, to the best of my knowledge, was not a twin. So, who is this man who talks and looks like him? The tears return.

'Please, calm down. The doctor says you should rest.'

How can I rest when my heart is on fire? I look at my son and daughter and it is obvious they are confused. Demilade is crying now and Ajoke is maintaining a stoic face.

'I want to see him. I need to ask him a few questions.'

'Unfortunately, he is not going to be around for some time. He has gone to Austin and will be there for three months.'

The tears return.

'Please, I need his contacts. I must speak with him for my sanity's sake.'

'Just rest. I need to seek his permission first.'

'Help me, please.'

'Ma'am, please you need to calm down,' Ismael says.

'I'm not crazy,' I say, then close my eyes to keep the tears in.

Back home after I return from the hospital, sleep eludes me. In my state of sleeplessness, my husband's love for a good argument makes me smile. I remember a day when my Omoniyi returned from a trip to Lagos.

'Everything there is messed up,' he said.

'Where are you talking about?' I asked.

'Where else but your Nigeria! Everything goes in that country. People lie to get into power and start giving excuses for their failure. If the country were a going concern, it would have been declared bankrupt and offered as scrap to interested parties.'

He kept quiet, and I thought he had finished, but he was only gathering steam.

'Five minutes after we started boarding, only a few of us were on board. The pilot began offering an apology to passengers pleading that they would need to wait for some passengers still stuck at the security zone.

'The types of things that happen at Nigeria's airports are scandalous. The other day, bandits invaded the runway and attacked a private jet. They stole from passengers and the crew. Jesus Christ, only in Nigeria! If bandits can invade airports, then we can forgive those operating on the streets. Then, of course, there was that time they had cattle on the runway.'

He went on to narrate his experiences with thieves on the streets of Lagos.

'So, I was going out and decided to go by public transport instead of taking a taxi. When I got to the car park, I stopped to buy something. I was about to pay when I felt a strange hand sliding into my pocket. I held the hand thinking that it was a familiar person. As I held the hand, I turned smiling; I encountered three strange faces. One of them moved close as if to hug me. Between us, he pointed a gun to my chest. The thing was rusty, locally made, but you never argue with the man with a gun. Those guys took my wallet containing my card and the twenty-five thousand naira I'd just withdrawn. I had a few dollars in there too. And those guys took my phone. I had to buy a palasa one to call you.'

'I'm glad you are okay and back to me in one piece.'

I asked him to let us pray but he had not finished.

'A middle-aged female passenger died inside one of the toilets at the airport. Moments before her death, the passenger suffered a bout of pain that made her rush to the toilet where she died. I am in shock,' he said.

'Pull yourself together. Death is no respecter of persons. It kills the good and leaves the bad and ugly to continue their havoc on humankind,' I said.

Before we slept that day we argued about his position that white people created problems for Africa.

'How?' I asked.

'They underdeveloped the nations of Africa, stole our resources and used the proceeds to develop their countries and now they are shutting the gates against us. Imagine the UK asking Nigerians to stay at home by frustrating visa issuance; I don't blame them, I blame those ignoramuses who call themselves our leaders.'

'Even though I agree with you to some extent, I think the blame is more with our leaders and even our people; a people get the leader they deserve,' I said.

'Really? Like you don't know that there is election rigging going on.'

'Yes, Omoniyimi, they rig elections in Nigeria. Elections are tampered with all over the world. But if more people go out to vote, and stand by to defend their votes, elections will be harder to rig,' I said.

'Stand by to defend their votes? And risk catching a bullet in the head. Babe, I have heard you.'

'Hmmn,' I said.

'Did I tell you what happened in Benin?' He said.

'What happened in Benin?' I asked.

'The ancient city was seized by red apparel-wearing chiefs, priests, witch doctors and sorcerers in a bid to purge and exorcise the city and its environs of bloodshed and prostitution. The purpose of the rituals was to activate deities, grooves, shrines, idols and other deified antiquities to rid the Benin Kingdom of the disheartening social strives that have desecrated the land and debased the humanity of the people.

'The Oba placed curses on all individuals promoting prostitution. The oaths many girls are made to swear before they are lured to Europe to hawk their flesh were broken. The monarch warned those aiding and abetting human trafficking through the use of black magic, subjecting their victims to the oaths of secrecy to desist or face the wrath of the gods and the ancestors of the land.'

I laughed and asked: 'So, has prostitution stopped there, now? Have more girls not been trafficked since then?'

'Many girls have regained their freedom since then. We need to believe our own things and stop relying on the Bible and Quran to save us. The oyinbos and Arabs only deceived us into accepting these faiths. They forced us to choose between the Bible and the gun and our fathers chose the Bible. We need to change as a people.'

I did not respond. I knew his take on colonialism, power and religion. I knew that when Omoniyi started on these topics, he never stopped. I did not say much as I loved to listen to his intellection. I was also tired and needed to sleep. As if on cue, he went into the bathroom, had a bath and snuggled close to me when he returned. No matter how heated or how mild our arguments were, we always ended them in bed.

Hours after my recollection, I stay awake and try to brainstorm on how to unravel the mystery that my life has become. The people who should have been able to help are long gone.

At the time I met Omoniyi, he had neither a father nor a mother. His father, he told me, died when he was four. His mother died in 2001, the year before we met in Houston and agreed to spend the rest of our lives together. He was an only child. He told me his maternal and paternal relatives were fetish, and he had never associated with them. They were cruel to his mother after his father's death. They took almost everything he owned and made him and his mother suffer.

I stare at the Olokun mask on the bedroom shelf. I bought it from an African art exhibition in Baltimore some years ago. The tears are gathering again, but I will not cry. Crying will not solve my problem.

My best bet remains James, that is what Ismael says his name is but three months is a long time for me to wait.

Did a nurse separate James and Omoniyi at birth after collecting money from a couple desperate for a baby? This question drags my mind far and near, but I have no answer. More queries flood my mind: Did the nurse lie to Omoniyi's parents that one of the twins died at birth? Was that why they never told Omoniyi he had a twin brother?

I stand from the bed, pick up Valium 5, swallow two tablets with water and sleep soon pays me a visit.

The following morning I knock on Ismael's door. I see the concern on his face immediately he opens the door and meets me.

'I have spoken with James and he is willing to meet you this weekend,' he says before I even greet.

'He will meet you here in my flat.'

'Thank you, but one more thing,' I say still standing.

'What?'

'You said you grew up with James in Ilupeju--'

'Yes.'

'What can you tell me about him?'

Ismael looks at me as if he will burst out laughing but quickly adjusts his mood.

'Please have a seat,' he says. 'Coffee? I have cream and sugar.'

'No, thank you,' I say.

He motions me to a two-seater by the plasma television. Pictures of his wife and kids dressed in Indian attire adorn the white walls. I wonder where they have all gone this early morning.

'James and I lived in the same house on Sura Mogaji Street in Ilupeju. If you know Ilupeju well, you will know it is home to Indians. There is even an Indian Language School, which I attended. James' father was our landlord, and even though we did not mix with Nigerians a lot, James and I were quite close. He wanted to follow his parents' paths, they were University professors, but they have since retired. He has three other siblings, two younger brothers and an older sister. I moved here with my parents after secondary school, but James and I remained in touch. My parents told me I was born in that house. That was two years after they moved to Nigeria from Durban. So that is it except there is something specific you want to know.'

I want to know if James and Omoniyi were twins. I want to know if they were separated. I want to know the circumstances. I want to know if it is just a mere resemblance. Like the Yoruba people believe we are created in twos. Is James my late husband's doppelgänger?

Ismael obviously cannot answer my questions. So, I let him be, thank him and return to my flat.

Back in the flat, I resolve that science is the only way out. A DNA test should be able to establish the truth. I have been told that any material taken from a man could be used to test for DNA. I decide that there must be something to use from my husband's toothbrush or his shaving stick. I decide that I will show James my husband's picture to get him to agree to a DNA test.

On Saturday morning, Ismael knocks on my door. I am excited and run to open the door because I know Ismael has come to inform me that James has arrived. When I open the door, Ismael is there, and there is no James.

'What happened?' I ask.

'He's dead. I just got a call that he's been in an accident. James is the only one who did not survive. He died on the spot.'

'I'm sorry,' I say.

'Yeah,' he says, 'I need to contact his family.'

I watch him go, but I feel raw. It feels like I am a widow again. I need no one to tell me that my quest has ended and the truth is dead. My questions will never be answered, as I slump, I tell myself I knew James was Omoniyi.

9

LYDIA'S WORLD

The day after Tunmininu died, Mama Demola called Lydia to break the news to her. The two of them had kept in touch since Demola's death. She screamed and was close to tears. The thought of anything happening to Demola Jnr, her only hope, made her cringe with fear. Long after Mama Demola dropped the call, she was still troubled, not by the death of her rival's son - Demola had had an affair which led to another child - but by a fact she recently stumbled upon.

Demola Jnr, Lydia's only child, had been ill. When he didn't seem to be getting better after all she had done, she took him to the hospital. A battery of tests was conducted and they included blood tests to establish his blood group and genotype. The results of the tests were puzzling to her; they showed that Demola Jnr's genotype was AS.

'It can't be. I am AA, and his father is AA. His delivery record given to us in the hospital after his birth also recorded his genotype as AA,' Lydia had told the doctor.

'It is nearly impossible to get blood tests wrong madam, but just so that you are sure we haven't made a mistake, we will rerun the tests. You may have a wrong record. I am sure you think that is impossible because this is the UK, but I can tell you that medical practitioners here are not immune to errors,' the doctor said.

And when a rerun of the test was done, it came out the same, and it got Lydia thinking. She was a virgin when she met and married Demola. Her puzzlement saw her doing internet searches to see if there was any chance of parents with AA genotype having a child with AS genotype. All her research confirmed what doctors told her. She would have to keep this information to herself until she was sure what the problem was. But her consolation was that she never slept with anyone other than Demola. There was a new man in her life, Roy. He came into the picture a few months ago.

My phone rang. I closed the book. Truecaller revealed the caller as Ogunmodede.

'Hello,' I said weakly.

'Can I talk to Mr Olukorede S. Yishau?' he said.

'Speaking...'

'Good afternoon sir...'

'Good afternoon. I am Professor Bunmi Ogunmodede from the University of Port Harcourt. I will like to invite you to the Literary Festival being hosted by the university in September. It will be an honour to have you read to us from your book, In the Name of Our Father. *Please text me your e-mail address so I will send you the details,' he said, even before I accepted.*

I had no reason to say no. So, I ended the call and sent my e-mail address. I felt thirsty, made for the fridge, grabbed a bottle of water and gulped it down my throat. I soon returned to Lydia's world.

Lydia was getting fond of Roy, a British lawyer and divorcee from East London. She had met gangling Roy at a Tesco store in Abbey Wood where she was an auditor. After minutes of staring at Demola Jnr's picture on the wall, she decided it was time to face her fears by involving a person she could trust. She thought of Roy. She thought of Jayden, her Jamaican friend and colleague at work. She ruled out Mama Demola. Although she trusted her, this was not the sort of matter she could bring to her attention. She settled for Roy and dialled his number. His phone rang out. She dialled again and left a message on the answering machine.

Hey Roy, please call back. It is pretty urgent.

A few minutes later, Roy called back.

'Hi Love, what is happening? Your message scared me,' Roy said.

'Could you please come over? It's not something I want to talk about on the phone.'

'Okay, give me a few minutes to clear my table,' Roy said.

It was a Saturday, and she was off work. Demola Jnr was at Jayden's to spend time with her son, Hank. Immediately she let Roy in; she said, 'I think there is a problem about Demola.'

'What problem could that be? I thought the doctors gave him an all-clear report two weeks ago after the crisis,' a confused Roy said, untying his red-and-pink-stripe tie and pulling off his black shoes.

The two of them sat on the couch. Roy stretched his arms and pulled her to him.

'There is a high possibility that he is not my son…'

'Whaaaat? How can that be?'

Lydia told him about the doctors' shocking find.

'That is serious,' Roy said, massaging her shoulders as if to take away some of the pressure.

They fell silent for a few minutes.

'What do you think I should do?'

'Where and in what hospital was he born?'

When she mentioned the name of the hospital, Roy screamed, 'That hospital is notorious. There was an enquiry into their activities recently, and it shows that there are all sorts of peculiar activities going on there. How it has remained open shocks me.'

Roy fiddled with his phone. Then he handed it to Lydia. 'Here. I pulled this off the internet.'

We found a lax approach to checking babies' name bands. The head of midwifery at the hospital did not have an explanation for this development, which means babies could easily be switched and mothers could have gone home with the wrong babies. We also found that the possibility the wrong medication was administered to one baby instead of another was high.

The hospital did not employ as many midwives as it required to ensure the birthing and post-delivery process of the hospital was supervised adequately.

Mothers told us that they are treated without regard or care. There were some intra-cultural issues and some bullying between midwives and patients. We also discovered that doctors and midwives referred to patients by their bed numbers rather than by name.

We were shocked to find grievous errors at Chapel Hospital, such as a surgeon leaving an object inside a patient after an operation, a dentist extracting a wrong tooth, patients getting the wrong diagnosis, and ultimately receiving the wrong medication.

There was a general lack of a safe and secure environment for new-born babies. Something urgent must be done to address the lapses.

Lydia was shaking by the time she finished reading the report. Roy held her tightly as the tears came.

'So, if Demola is not my son, where is my son?'

'You don't know that for certain, but you need to find out,' Roy said.

'How?'

'First, you need to get a DNA test done. That way, you'll know if Demola is your child or not,' Roy said.

'Roy, what are you saying?'

'If Demola is yours, then Demola Snr was not the father,' Roy said.

'What? Are you by any means insinuating…'

'Calm down. It's either that or somebody lied about his genotype.'

'I am scared, Roy!'

'You will have to maintain a clear head. But in the meantime, get the samples ready as soon as Demola comes back home. We'll go to the hospital first thing tomorrow to get that test done.'

Lydia was not herself throughout the night. She walked to Demola's room every few minutes and looked at him. Willing herself to see something definite in his features that told her he was hers. She willed for something – a curve on the lip maybe, or a shape of the nose, but she saw nothing that she did not already know. Her son's features were the same as she had known them since he was placed on her belly as a baby and told 'this is your son.' How now could she seek truth in something she had never doubted? Especially when suspicion was messing with her sense of judgement.

What if Demola wasn't hers? She thought. Would she tell him? What would it mean for a boy who had known no other parent for most of his life? But then, what would the knowledge do to her? Would she love the boy? Then, she thought. What if the boy was hers? How would she go about obtaining answers from the dead? What would that news do to the family? Would her late husband's family reject her? And maybe strip her of all her husband's belongings? Would she become a free woman, without any attachments? And what would she do when the boy became old enough and wanted to know about his father? Would she say, *my son, I am your mother, but your father is not your father? By the time we could have confirmed he had passed away from the reach of facts and left us with only uncertainties?*

That night was perhaps the longest one in Lydia's life. The more she willed daybreak to come, the longer the night seemed. Eventually, she gave up on sleep and turned to do some research on the internet. She found a December 2016 *Telegraph* report on The Royal London Hospital titled 'Maternity Ward Chaos Leaves Mothers at Risk of Going Home with the Wrong Baby, Report Finds'. She would have argued that the U.K with her vast security and surveillance systems could not be home to such anomaly. But there it was. Reading the report, she found that the hospital had been forced to make changes. But there was still a chance that three in one thousand babies could be switched at birth.

The next morning, she woke up at 4am, said a long-winded prayer to God to make the hospital confirm Demola as her son. Then she got him ready for school. By 7am, she was seated, fully dressed, waiting for Roy, who would not arrive till 10am.

When Roy arrived, he met Lydia on the couch, fully dressed, asleep, a framed picture of Demola clutched to her chest. Roy looked around Lydia's immaculate surroundings. The big living room painted cream, the coffee brown upholstery, the chocolate rug and the heavy glass centre table. His eyes went to the painting of a woman breastfeeding a child on the wall, and he wanted to ask the woman in the painting what she knew, but he stopped. Lydia had stirred.

'Lydia,' Roy said kindly. 'Baby, wake up.'

Lydia awoke. She tried to smile, but it was more of a grimace. 'How long have you been around?' she asked.

'Long enough to know that you did not sleep at night.'

'Look at him, Roy. He is my son. Look at the resemblance.'

Roy gently collected the framed picture and laid it down. He hugged Lydia and said kindly: 'Babe, I know this is not easy for you. But you have to know. Let's go to the hospital. I've booked an appointment.'

'Thank you,' Lydia said, 'I could not have done this without you.'

My phone rang again. This time, it was my immediate younger sister, Bukola. We had not spoken for some time. As I tried to pick the call, it rang out. I called back and all I got was: 'The number you are calling is not available at the moment. Please try again later.' I dropped the phone and returned to the drama of Lydia's life. I put the phone on silent mode and threw it on the dining table. I wanted to read the story in peace.

The result eventually came and Lydia's prayers were not answered. The boy she and her late husband named Demola Jnr was not theirs. The truth brought tears to her eyes, and it took Roy a lot of effort to get her back into the car.

While driving home, Roy knew what to do next. He would write to Chapel Hospital, intimating its management of the fact that there was a baby swap in the hospital. He would get the details about Demola's birth from Lydia and write the letter immediately.

Demola Jnr was not yet back from school when they got home, so it was easy getting all the required details and writing the letter without a curious child wanting to know what was happening and getting more curious if he received clipped answers. Roy dispatched the letter, which was on his law firm's letterhead, the same day with a clear threat to sue the hospital if no reply was given on time. He attached a copy of the DNA result.

Roy was still with Lydia when Demola Jnr arrived from school and he could see how she struggled to contain her emotions.

'Mum, no hug?' Demola Jnr said.

'Sorry, baby. I have a boil in my armpit.'

'Sorry, Mum', the boy said. He had a look of pity on his face. Suddenly, he asked, 'Does it hurt?'

'Yes, baby, it hurts.'

'Sorry,' the boy said and ran to hold Lydia around the waist. Tears stood in Lydia's eyes, but she blinked them away. Suddenly, the boy left her and turned to Roy, 'I don't want to hurt Mummy.'

Roy left not long after the scene. No sooner had Roy left, Lydia rushed into Demola Jnr's room and gathered him into a hug.

'Has the boil gone so soon?' he asked her.

'Shh, shhhh… Mummy loves you. I am your mummy, and I love you,' Lydia said.

Two weeks later, a letter from the Chapel Hospital confirmed that Demola Jnr was not hers. There had indeed been a mistaken switch. It had happened with the only other black boy born that day, and the hospital had been able to trace him to the Republic of Benin where his mother was serving on a Christian Missionary Board.

Three weeks later, Lydia, Roy and Susan Welsh, a medical doctor at Chapel Hospital, were on their way to Kpedekpo community in Benin Republic, where Mrs Maduemesi, the birth mother of Demola Jnr, and Johnwest, Lydia's real son, had been living for one year.

The hospital had contacted Mrs. Maduemesi through the UK High Commission in Benin Republic but gave no details. An official of the High Commission, Anne Wesley, joined them in Benin Republic from where they headed to Kpedekpo, a land notorious for raising children for export to Nigeria as house helps.

They met Mrs Maduemesi at an orphanage in the community. She received them warmly, but there was something strange and sombre about her appearance. She wore a black gown. Lydia looked for a sign of a boy who would look like her or Demola. Then she saw a picture on the wall and did not doubt in her mind that this was her son. His resemblance to Demola was beyond doubt. She smiled, and her heart beat faster.

The High Commission's official, who Lydia did not bother to ask her name, explained why they were there to Mrs. Maduemesi, who burst into tears.

'Why are you crying madam?'

'I lost the boy you are talking about.'

Lydia jumped off her seat and came to where Mrs Maduemesi was sitting. Roy walked up to Lydia and held her.

'He was bitten by a snake and died before we could get help,' Mrs Maduemesi said and broke down in tears.

'If you go inside, you will see some women from the village who have come to keep me company. It is because I am mourning him that I am in black. So, are you people saying my own child is somewhere in London?'

Lydia was already on the ground. She was not prepared for this. What she had planned for was how to make it up to her son whom this woman and her husband named Johnwest. Now, he was dead.

'When the High Commission contacted me, Johnwest was still alive. And I was not even told the reason for the call. They simply said to expect visitors. Please, are you saying I have a child in London?'

Susan answered in the affirmative and Lydia collapsed on the floor, not sure whether to cry or laugh.

'I will need to see him,' she said, as Roy led Lydia back to the car that brought them.

'Please come to Cotonou tomorrow; the High Commission will arrange for you to return home and do a DNA test with the boy and we will know what to do after we get the results.'

Lydia lost it on the way back to Cotonou. She had to be restrained from jumping out of the car. She was closely monitored on the flight back to London. She did not go home on arrival, she did not get to see Demola, she did not get the chance to tell him she loved him, and he was hers; she spent the next few months in a psychiatric home. While there, her popular refrain was 'Demola is my son. I might not be his mother, but I am his mummy. Demola is my son. I might not be his mother, but I am his mummy.' She said this every day from sunup to sundown. She was not violent. She was simply busy trying to win an argument against herself and against fate, which had dealt her a tricky hand.

There were tears in my eyes by the time I finished this story. I had to remind myself that I had just read a piece of fiction. I dried my tears, but for weeks Lydia, Roy, DNA and death went with me, everywhere.

10

OPEN WOUND

It was Uthman Dan Fodio who described me as an open wound, which only the truth can heal. Most of you humans know me as the conscience. I am in all of you. I can never leave; can never be exorcised. No amount of prayers or palliatives can kill me. If anyone succeeds in silencing me, it is only for a while. And that takes a lot of work because I always come back stronger.

In the last few months, I have been busy working on one of you. Her name is Dazini, daughter of Madumere, widow of late Colonel Edward Dibiana and baby mama of Moses.

All her children, yes, the two of them are not her late husband's. They belong to Moses; he is their father.

This is how it happened.

They met by accident. It was accidental because Dazini was involved in an accident, Moses helped her, and they became close and closer until they started hitting the sack.

After the accident, when Dazini was in the hospital, Moses became a permanent feature by her bedside. The accident occurred on the eve of her 18th birthday. She was returning from a visit to a friend on Ikwerre Road. Her dad gave her money for a cab, but she chose to take a bus for the experience, she had never been on one. It was regretful: the driver of the bus was drunk; they ran into a ditch and the bus somersaulted.

Dazini woke up three days later at Dorcas Egede Hospital. The first thing that greeted her was the pain that shot through her body when she tried to sit up. When her eyes focused, she saw a boy about her age standing by her bed, looking concerned. The boy took one look at her and hurried off. He returned with her parents in tow. They were the ones who shouted to attract the doctor.

Her father introduced the boy as Moses, her benefactor. Moses came out from a crowd of onlookers and noticed she was unconscious while the other passengers were groaning. He carried her, called a taxi and rushed her to the hospital. The hospital staff had called her father after rummaging through her purse. He was the only other person, apart from her parents, who visited her every day, staying for about one hour each day.

He was there on the day she was discharged. He was there when the family rejoiced that she survived. They allowed him in the car that took the whole family home. The family thanked him for his kindness and prayed God's blessing upon him. When Moses and Dazini started getting close, everyone watched with interest because the best friendships always started in strange circumstances. God works in mysterious ways, wonders are His to perform. But one day, when Moses came to Dazini's house when her parents were at work and put his left hand on her shoulder and looked into her eyes with some longing, she brushed his hand off roughly and hissed. He departed quietly.

Dazini's mother had warned her about boys and what danger they could pose to her life. But she hadn't been bothered about Moses because he was a benefactor and she always heard him and Dazini arguing about school stuff and news.

After the shoulder touching incident, Moses stopped visiting. Dazini wasn't bothered much at first, but she soon started to miss him. She jumped almost every time she heard the gate open. She wished it was him every time someone knocked on the door. She struggled with her thoughts. She did not seem to understand what was going on with her.

Dazini's parents noticed that Moses was no longer coming to the house. They asked if there had been a misunderstanding and Dazini answered in the negative. She did not tell her parents what he did and how she reacted. One day, her mother asked if she knew his house, and she said yes. Then, she encouraged Dazini to go and find out why Moses stopped coming to their house.

'He may even be ill,' she said. 'We ought to know that all is well with him.'

Before I could jump on this piece of information to tilt Dazini's thoughts one way or another, she had gone off in search of Moses at the Ikwerre Road room-and-parlour apartment he lived in with his mother. Fortunately, the woman was not at home when Dazini got there. Moses' sitting room boasted a small television, a transistor radio, a two-seater couch and a cane wardrobe with books she guessed belonged to Moses.

A rush of emotion overtook her when she saw him. She was happy he was well. She had been troubled since her mother suggested all might not be well with him. Seeing him in perfect condition warmed Dazini's heart.

'Why did you stop coming to our house?' Dazini asked after the pleasantries.

Moses did not speak. He gave her that look that seemed to be saying: 'Ask yourself.'

'My mum was worried about you and asked me to come and

see that you are okay,' Dazini said, expecting him to make some comments, but he just kept staring at her like some expensive jewellery.

When Dazini saw that he was still angry with her, she decided to explain why she did not take kindly to his inappropriate touch. She spoke about what her mother had told her about boys. Moses apologised and said he just suddenly became drawn to her and did not even know when he touched her shoulder. Dazini accepted the apology and was glad that she had her friend back.

Dazini returned home after an hour and reported to her mother that Moses was well and stayed away because he was busy. Something in Dazini did not want to give her mother any detail that could make her bar Moses from coming to the house.

Days passed and Moses still didn't visit. Dazini's mother did not bother to ask again since she had lied about why he did not come to the house. The day she decided to go looking for him again was the day he showed up. Dazini's mother was about going to her supermarket at the time. She was the one who opened the door for him.

'Long time Moses,' Dazini's mother said on letting him in.

'Good morning, ma,' he greeted and found a space on the three-seater chair.

'It's good to see you again. How are your parents?'

Moses smiled. 'Fine, ma.'

'Alright, take care. I am off to the market,' she said and rushed out.

With mother gone and the two of them alone, she pounced on him: 'What is your problem Moses? I explained to you and you said you understood.'

'I did. I was only busy,' he said, obviously not being truthful.

'Too busy for me? The same me you saw every day until I protested your inappropriate touching of my shoulder.'

He looked away so Dazini would not see the tears welling up in his eyes. He blinked repeatedly

'Don't do that, Moses,' she pleaded.

Dazini moved closer to him and held his right hand. She knew there was a pull dragging her to him, and she needed to resist it. She needed to listen to her mother's advice about boys and their evil ways.

'You are my friend, a great friend of mine. I cherish you and respect you. I only do not want us to complicate things,' Dazini said, but deep down her, she could not vouch that things would not get complicated.

Her heartbeat increased the more she held his hand. God, what is happening to me, she thought. She withdrew her hand from his and went to the kitchen. She brought some rice and a soft drink for him to eat. At first, he didn't want to take it, but he ate the food when he saw the expression on her face.

After the meal, Dazini asked him: 'What do you really want from me?' He had no answer for her and she pleaded with him to let them go back to the pre-shoulder touching era.

Dazini saw him off after some minutes and returned home disturbed. About an hour after, there was a knock at the door. She opened the door, and there he was.

'I want to spend more time with you,' he said.

Dazini let him in and they shared gist like old times. Two hours and some minutes later, he announced his departure. She saw him off and said: 'Go home this time around.'

They laughed and parted ways. But as days turned to weeks and weeks into months, the butterfly in Dazini's stomach kept developing. Moses was not helping matters. He was visiting almost every day and if he did not show up on a particular day, Dazini would feel bad.

I, Dazini's conscience, saw the direction of her thoughts and started to tug at her heartstrings. One time, Moses stayed away for two days and Dazini was beside herself. When he showed up, she hugged him. When he asked for another hug, she obliged. I know from that singular experience that emotions can temporarily overpower knowledge. But when knowledge returns, it comes with all the weight I can lend it.

To make a long story short, they became lovers. Moses was a smart boy with rascally traits. His words and actions were music to Dazini's ears. He could do no wrong. Their connection was something I could not explain. Every time I tried to channel Dazini's thoughts, I met Moses right there in her heart. She had given him a throne and he had turned it into a palace. Moses took over her heart and started to possess her dreams. I watched.

There was a day they were walking on a road in Eleme, and a boy threw a stone at Dazini. She screamed like the world was coming to an end. Moses was enraged. He dealt the boy some blows and asked him to apologise before letting him go. Dazini looked at him that day like he was a god.

The first time they had sex, they did it in the afternoon in Dazini's parents' house when nobody else was around. Moses had come visiting and Dazini was in the kitchen listening to him talk as he stood by the door. Suddenly, she felt Moses' hand under her blouse, making its way to her breasts. She turned to tell him to stop, but he kissed her.

I flashed the image of her mother and played the wise instructions about boys and their evil in her mind, it did not work.

Minutes later, Dazini's blouse lay on the floor. Moses' clothes were strewn on the kitchen counter. They stood in their birthday suits; excitement etched all over their faces. Despite the scent of cooking food, they took to each other and danced to the music of passion. Dazini would days later remember how she rested her back against the fridge while Moses moved. How she perched on the edge of the kitchen table. How she leaned on the stool. She would remember that after it was all done, she was giddy and happy and in love so much so she felt her heart would burst. She would marvel days later at how sensible she had been to clean the fridge and areas she touched in the throes of passion. She would try to caution herself not to lean on the fridge and moan. And in-between that giddiness of thought, Moses came in regularly when her parents were not around, and they re-enacted their passion until the bombshell fell one morning.

Dazini discovered she was pregnant two months after her first tryst with Moses. It was the day before her admission letter arrived by mail from Georgetown University in the U.S. Together, Moses and Dazini went to a doctor in a remote part of Port Harcourt and she had an abortion.

Dazini arrived in Washington DC on a Tuesday morning. Washington was a small city at the time. It blew her mind. Port Harcourt, her home, was beautiful — but not in the sense of Washington. Washington, depending on where you were, could be lovely, dangerous or dirty. When people drove in Downtown Washington, their doors and windows were locked. The crime rate was always on the increase in Downtown Washington. Alongside the finesse of government work, there were also crack cocaine, murder and gang wars. Many inner-city neighbourhoods still showed the effects of the 1968 riots.

During her first week in DC, the novice in her showed itself and she had a knife pulled on her. She had intervened on behalf of a prostitute running from her pimp. The pimp who was not humoured by the intervention pulled a knife. She almost peed herself.

Graffiti was a big part of the culture in this district under the watch of Ronald Reagan as president of the United States and Marion Barry as the beloved mayor. A renowned artist Cool 'Disco' Dan's tag was all over the city. Dazini loved the graffiti.

Erol's Video Club was where residents rented VHS during the weekends to burn time. Dazini joined the video club's queue from time to time. She was also part of the prime years for Georgetown basketball and was excited when John Thompson's team made it to the finals three times and won the National Championship in 1984. Her interest in basketball was sharpened at Lexington Camp.

On several occasions, she ran into homeless people on 14th St and P St and could not believe it. There was even a couple she saw. They had paper cups on the ground and cigarette wrappers and urine and bottles.

As the oldest Catholic and Jesuit-affiliated institution of higher education in the United States, her school, Georgetown University was rigorous and global in perspective. It afforded her the exciting opportunity to take advantage of Washington, D.C. She had a great time seeing dance, plays, concerts, and participating in student clubs and organisations. Off-campus, Dazini visited museums, theatres, concert halls and famous monuments and landmarks.

She loved its fountains, large clusters of flowers, groves of trees and open quadrangles. She spent a lot of time admiring its elevated site above the Potomac River overlooking Northern Virginia. With Medinat Kanab, her first real friend at Georgetown, Dazini roamed the campuses in their free periods. The main gates, known as the

Healy Gates, located at the intersection of 37th and O Streets played host to them on many occasions. They visited all of its historical sites, such as the Healy Hall, Gaston Hall, Riggs Library, the Bioethics Library Hirst Reading Room and the Georgetown University Astronomical Observatory.

Dazini would never forget the trouble she went through on account of Medinat's insatiable appetite for sex. She ran into a problem in their second year when she got pregnant. Because of its Jesuit affiliation, Georgetown was pro-life. The university's Medical Centre and Georgetown University Hospital were prohibited from performing abortions.

Dazini had to accompany Medinat downtown to seek out a pliant doctor who helped her remove the foetus. The doctor's clinic was in a neighbourhood where drug lords hawked their wares in the open and fights broke out at the slightest provocations.

After the abortion, Medinat did not learn her lesson. She continued hopping from bed to bed. 'Sex is therapy; the fastest way to get over a guy is to get under another one,' she would tell Dazini each time she asked her to slow down.

'You will not die if you don't have it,' Dazini would say, but Medinat would just laugh it off.

Dazini was not exactly a saint at Georgetown. Initially, she found herself unable to get Moses out of her mind and her interest in video films, basketball and sight-seeing were her ways of dumping Moses in her past. Moses had no money to give her, but she was pleased with what he had to offer. Now was the time to move on and she was willing to do everything to get over him.

After a year in DC, Dazini started a relationship with a white boy, Joel. Joel was handsome. He was the sort you can describe as beautiful despite being a boy. They hit it off on a good note. Like

Dazini, he was from a well-to-do home and they cruised about Washington in his Mercedes Benz coupe.

All was well until the day they decided to take things beyond cruising about in his car and having dinners and lunches in choice restaurants. It was in her room. Medinat was under the weather and her parents had come to take her to the hospital. They had the room to themselves. A video of Marvin Gaye's 'Sexual Healing' caused the fire to burn inside the two of them. Joel made the first move. He tried kissing her and she opened her mouth and closed her eyes to savour the sweetness and texture of his tongue.

One minute into the kiss, Dazini started seeing Moses' face. She just could not feel Joel. She tried to block out Moses and see if she would enjoy the kissing and the caressing. It did not work. Their making out on the couch did not work the kind of miracle she was used to. When eventually they made it to the bed and Joel took off her lace panties and started thrusting into her, slowly at first, then firmly and urgently, it all felt bland. At least for her. When eventually he shuddered and fell on her, her 'thank God' collided with his 'thank you'. She did not orgasm.

For Dazini, that was it. She stopped seeing him after that day. He asked what he did wrong and she refused to injure his ego by telling him the truth. He cried. He fell sick. He contemplated suicide before his friends called him to order. He wrote her a letter saying sex with her was the best he had ever had. But Dazini was done, her heart was not in it.

Dazini concentrated on her studies and never had another relationship until she returned to Nigeria. It was not long after she returned that she met Olola Akioye. Tall, handsome and mixed-race Olola was working with an oil drilling firm. He was the deputy managing director of the firm owned by foreigners.

Charming, disarming and a great speaker, he did not have to do much before Dazini said yes to his love advances. She needed to date again. It had been long since she felt like a woman.

Her mother fell for his charm too and she gladly called him 'my son'. They became inseparable. They had lunch together every working day. Their offices were just a few minutes apart.

In the sixth month of their relationship, Dazini started getting worried that Olola was not asking for sex. She could not understand why. But because she was in Nigeria where women were trained to be shy about such issues, she restrained herself. When she couldn't handle it any longer, she decided to act by kissing him. He did not resist and it was good, really good. Trouble, however, arose when she tried to take it further. He resisted her attempt to touch his penis and that worried her. She did not ask why. She simply let him be.

A week later, in his three-bedroom official apartment, they became intimate again. For all of the twenty minutes of passionate kissing, there was no bulge in his trousers. As Dazini attempted to touch it for confirmation, he resisted again. She could not take it any longer.

'What is the problem, Olola?' Dazini asked.

'Nothing,' he said, widening the distance between them.

'Why are you stopping me from touching you?'

He pretended not to hear her. She was horny already and all she wanted was action and not talk.

'I need to go and see someone,' he said and made to stand up.

'If you stand up Olola, forget this relationship,' she threatened.

He returned to the seat and after about one minute, he started talking: 'Before you, I have had several relationships, and once I had sex with the ladies, they repulsed me. I love you and don't want that to change. I think we should wait until our wedding night. My Christian faith also is against it.'

Dazini would have believed him, but she knew he was lying because he had invoked Christianity. Olola was not even a churchgoer, not to talk of being a born-again Christian. She was convinced there was something he was hiding and she intended to find out.

'Okay, but I noticed that there was no bulge in your trouser while we were necking,' she said.

He did not even waste time before telling her a practised lie.

'Of course, it is because I have zeroed in my mind that I did not want to go too far. There is something called self-control. I am saving the best for you.'

He maintained a straight face after giving this excuse. In order not to appear like a bad lady, Dazini decided not to push it again, but she was determined to find out the truth before committing herself. They went on for two more months without discussing the matter again. She also avoided trying to kiss him.

Her quest to find out the truth was one she did not know how to go about, but luck ran into her one day when a lady accosted her at the Ugwuanyi and Sons Supermarket on Okere Ugborikoko Street. She pleaded with her to listen to her and she obliged. She looked decent and she had no cause to doubt her. She told Dazini she had been seeing her and Olola together and wanted to know if they were dating. She said yes and the next thing she said shocked her.

'I am sure he would have told you he does not like having sex before the wedding night.'

She looked at Dazini's reaction.

'My sister, that man is not a man. Run before he turns you to a miserable woman.'

Before Dazini could say anything, the lady had left. She was transfixed for minutes not knowing whether to go into the supermarket or return home. She eventually returned home and tabled the matter before her mother. She also told her mother what had happened previously.

'You need to find out the truth,' her mother said.

'How?'

'You need to confront him and let him know that without confirmation of his manliness, you are going to end the relationship. Let him know that you believe he is lying,' her mother said.

Dazini saw sense in what her mother said and quickly went to his house. Lucky enough, he was home and she wasted no time in telling him all. To her surprise, he just broke down in tears and told her he had not had an erection in the last five years. He told her of the efforts he had made to correct the situation, including trips to specialists abroad.

'None of them has been able to explain what the problem is,' he said, tears cascading down his cheeks again.

Dazini felt pity for him but wondered why he was ridiculing himself by dating. As though he could read her mind, he said: 'People were calling me a eunuch and I needed to start dating to counter that view of me.'

He launched into another round of crying and Dazini was tempted to join in, but she felt angry that he was using her to create a wrong impression. She left him after some minutes and never returned.

It was not long after Dazini left Olola that she met Colonel Edward Dibiana. His first marriage had failed, but he had three kids to show for it. That was enough assurance for Dazini that he was a man. They married a little over a year later.

One year after they got married, she was yet to become pregnant and she became worried. They had sex as time permitted, but it just did not result in what she wanted.

'I am worried about your inability to get pregnant,' her husband complained one day.

Dazini was taken aback.

'What do you mean by that?'

Before he could say anything further, she added: 'Are you not the one who is supposed to get me pregnant? Be a man and do your duty.'

One week after this quarrel, Dazini decided to go and see a gynaecologist. She had planned to go with her husband, but he turned her down. His reason: It was her problem and she should solve it. He pointed at the fact that he had kids from his previous marriage to back his belief that the problem could not have been from him.

Dr. Adeola Akinremi, who attended to her at the Warri Specialist Hospital, was very polite. He asked questions nobody else would have asked, and she answered them all. When he asked her if she had been pregnant before, she was glad her husband was not there to hear her answer the question truthfully. He was worried about where she did the evacuation and asked her to run some tests.

The hospital had a fantastic laboratory, so she did not have to go out for the tests. She returned to see the doctor one week after and the cheerful way he received her told her there was no cause for alarm.

'I have gone through the tests' results and there is absolutely no reason why you should not conceive once you are having sex with a virile man,' he said. 'I'd like to see your husband to run some tests on him too.'

Dazini's heart was heavy because she felt the tests must have gotten something wrong. Her husband, for all she cared, had proved himself by having children from his previous marriage. Not one.

Not two. But three. 'The problem must be with me,' she concluded.

At home, Dazini briefed her husband about what the doctor said. When she asked him if he would see the doctor, he flared up and accused her of wanting to subject him to ridicule. For the first time since she married him, she queried his literacy. What educated man would see running a fertility test as ridicule?

Dazini cried for days but managed to appear like an iron lady at work. Her subordinates both loved and revered her and she did not want them to see her as a weakling.

For weeks, their home experienced a cold war. She returned to the hospital to brief Dr Akinremi. Even though he did not expressly say it, she had a feeling he was disappointed that her husband could take such a stand.

That night after leaving the hospital, she began to wonder if all was well with her husband, but his children from his previous marriage were evidence to the contrary. It also occurred to her that the problem could have arisen without him knowing years after having those kids. Dazini was confused and kept to herself. Even though they slept on the same bed, they were strangers. He had a big ego and he would not allow it to be touched. She saw him as a selfish man, who would not mind her just warming his bed because he already had kids from another woman.

Dazini began to loathe him. But she also wanted a child, so she continued sleeping with him. One day he saw her praying for a child and he joined her. Another time, he saw her watching a televangelist asking women looking for the fruit of the womb to touch their tummy and pray fervently, he joined in and she loved him for it.

It did not take time before Dazini put behind her any thought of him having any medical challenge. Somehow, the loathing disappeared. They got their groove back, travelled the world together and lived without care. He pampered her and played more than the role of a husband. He was also like her father and she was glad for this and it made her love him the more.

The paradise Dazini thought she had created with her husband collapsed when she ran into Moses, whom she had not seen for years. He was a politician in Cross River State and was at that time exploring the possibility of becoming a local government chairman. He insisted that they had dinner. Since her husband was not in town, she felt there was nothing wrong with having dinner with an old friend. They agreed to meet at the Presidential Hotel at 7pm.

By 7pm, Dazini met him waiting for her at the reception of the hotel.

'Gentleman,' she said on seeing him already waiting for her.

'You don't keep a lady waiting,' he said and led her to the Chinese restaurant.

They had an excellent dinner, dotted with animated conversations, spurts of laughter and too much red wine. When the dinner was over, Moses would not allow her to leave. He pleaded that she should follow him to his room upstairs.

'What do you want to tell me upstairs that you cannot tell me here?' she asked him. She was already a bit tipsy.

As he tried to raise his hand to plead his case further, his hand mistakenly touched her left breast and she simply died. She could feel a familiar but strange sensation all over her body. In that instant, memories of the past came flooding. She tried to block them out, reminding herself that she was now married and should allow such memories to die.

'Please don't say no,' he said, breaking into her thought.

He led the way, and she followed. I, Dazini's conscience, tried to remind her of her vows, but her body was screaming yes, yes, yes. I tried to prick her heart, but her body was in the way.

They had hardly locked the room when their lips married and their fingers explored the contours of each other's body. They soon became musicians singing songs that made sense to only them. He had her from the front. He took her from the back. Dazini sat on him and did the twin bounce. He even suspended her at some point. She felt she hadn't had it better since she got married.

She woke up the next morning, extremely happy, with a rhythm in her head and blues in her heart. She felt like a woman, a real woman. She had not felt like that in a long time.

Signs that Moses was going to be a permanent feature in her life started emerging when she discovered she was pregnant a month after their steamy session. Even though she was not sure who was responsible at that time, she was glad to have a baby to call her own. She told herself that the baby was her husband's. Didn't they make love three days after her session with Moses? When Dazini informed her husband that she was pregnant, the man was excited. I am a man, he said over and over, punching the air.

When the baby came, he was over the moon as though he had never seen a baby before. He looks just like me; he said—my carbon copy.

Two years and numerous sex sessions with her husband after, Dazini did not take in another child. She tried not to be worried. The third and fourth year soon rolled by and there was no other baby. Toni was growing and looking rather different from her husband. Though there was no medical examination, something told her Edward had become sterile. She could not ask him to go for a check-up, because she knew that he would point to Toni and say, 'there is the evidence you need. Or where did you get him from?'

Before Dazini knew it, Toni was six years old and still no other child. It was around this time she started to get seriously worried. It was also around this time that she ran into Moses again.

Dazini ran into Moses when she was part of a delegation sent by her company, Scodies Oil, to the Cross River State Government House. Moses was there in his capacity as Special Adviser to the Governor on Commerce. He maintained his composure throughout the meeting, while a storm raged in Dazini. When they broke for lunch, he sent an aide to give her his card with a short note that said *Please call*.

That night, alone in her room, she called him. Moses picked on the fourth ring.

'Hello,' Moses said, confidently.

'Hello,' Dazini answered. 'The last I knew you were trying to be Local Government Chairman.'

'Yes,' Moses answered. 'Been there, done that.' He exploded into a guffaw. When he quietened down, he said seriously. 'So, you just disappeared. Why? Why do you keep running away from me?'

'I wanted to concentrate on my husband and child,' Dazini said.

'How many babies do you have now?'

'One, but God will send us another one soon.'

Before he could say anything further, she added: 'I did not want you to distract me. I did not want trouble in my husband's house.'

Moses laughed and waited for Dazini to continue, but she chose to say nothing.

'We need to meet,' he said after the brief silence.

'Why, Moses?'

'For old times' sakes…'

'You are not serious,' she said and tried to laugh it off. 'By the way, how many children do you have now?'

His answer sent shock waves down her spine.

'Four.'

'So, you took going to replenish the earth as a personal project?'

Moses laughed. 'Please, our fathers had dozens of children.'

Dazini laughed too but said nothing. She wanted more children.

They spoke some more and agreed to meet at the GRA in Calabar. The story was not any different from what happened when they last met. They wined, dined and ended up in bed. Not long after, she discovered she was pregnant. Dazini was convinced that Moses was the father of Toni and the one in her womb. She also knew that it was a truth that she would never share. It was a secret she would carry to the grave.

Moses was imprisoned two months ago for the murder of his wife. He killed her after he discovered that two of her children were not his. His story made the headlines of major newspapers in the country. AIDE TO THE GOVERNOR CONVICTED OF MURDER one of the headlines screamed. Another newspaper header branded him the Killer Aide. Of course, the journalists did their homework and dredged into Moses' political journey. Dazini was afraid at the time that the journalists may eventually unearth the connection between her and Moses. But they were only concerned with his political trajectory and the implications of his conviction for his principal, the governor.

Even though the journalists did not link them together, I, as her conscience, have started pricking Dazini. And I have friends. One of them is memory. So recently, I drilled into one of those times that she attended church or watched a televangelist and I unearthed a statement: *The truth shall set you free.*

I shall continue pricking her until she confesses, to Moses, to her late husband's family, to her parents and then to God. I am not concerned about what happens to her externally when she makes this confession. I only care about the truth and Dazini's freedom.

A CONVERSATION IN SECRET WITH OLUKOREDE S. YISHAU

In this interview with Tope Salaudeen-Adegoke, Yishau discusses some aspects of the book.

Congrats on your latest book, *Vaults of Secret*, scheduled for release on the first of October. It is a significant date in the of history of Nigeria. I suppose it's not a coincidence for your book release?

Of course, it is not a coincidence. I had to beg my publisher to do me the honour of releasing the book to the public on that day and I am glad she obliged me. Picking the date is like killing two birds with one stone. One, I wanted to identify with our nation, a victim of secrets being kept by men and women who have had the chance to lead it. Two, my parents got married on October 1st some fifty years ago. For some reasons, my father also died on October 1st and it will be eight years we lost him this year. So, picking the date is to honour his memory and to honour my mother and my siblings, who October 1st means more than just Independence Day to.

The book is your first collection of short fiction, compared to your debut novel, *In the Name of Our Father*, what the

differences or features of the form do you personally find remarkable or challenging? I mean, how do you see short story form in terms of setting and character development?

Let me answer this question this way: the major difference, for me, between the short story and the novel is like living in a room apartment and living in a mansion. A family living in a room and the one living in a mansion have to enjoy life within their means. The family in mansion has more rooms, swimming pools and other facilities which the family in a room do not have, but life must go on. For me, a short story is like the family living in a room apartment. They must live within their means and manage to do everything essential; they must avoid frivolities. The family in the mansion is like the novel and they have more to explore. You have to be very disciplined with character development in a short story because there is no room for too much details; conflicts must be resolved within the available ambience. It is not particularly easy to write because I remember we kept going back and forth at the editing stage. A novel can afford to give more details and all that.

As the title suggests, the underlying theme in the book is secret. It's an important phenomenon of human nature because almost everybody has a secret, be it a fault or weakness or shame we try to conceal from others. What is your take on this?

Secrets are what we all cannot do without. Even people who say their lives are open books still have stuff they do not want to share with the public. Some people can even go to the extreme to have their secret kept.

It seems those who wield some form of power over us then are the ones with our secrets, whether we entrust it to them willingly or unwillingly, do you agree secret is also a form of power? I think this is more apparent in the story 'This Special Gift'. Through the narrator's eyes, a reader could bear witness to the perversion of power and the secret some powerful people live in the ultra rich parts of Lagos.

There is absolutely no doubt that he who has access to your secret, especially those who stumble on your secret like Emmanuel, can wield enormous power over you and we have seen instances where people use their access to secrets as a weapon of extortion or as a weapon to get undue advantage in a competitive situation.

I will like to add that both the rich and the poor harbour secrets that can be used against them, but the rich are the ones who have something to protect and as such will go to any extent to have their secrets permanently locked away in vaults buried deep in the Atlantic Ocean.

In as much as having access to a secret can be a weapon, it can also expose you to danger because when you have access to the secrets of the rich and powerful, chances are that they might also be after you. Probably some have been killed because of secrets they stumbled on, which they do not necessarily plan to use against the rich, but the need for preservation can make them do the extreme. So, I see it as a double-edged sword because while you can use it to your advantage, it can also be used as a reason for you to deserve death from hot lead.

Still on the story, I think one of the characters found out disposition is imitative of the conscience of some Nigerians who immediately blame someone else for their error – usually

the devil. Could you speak more on that since it's also a theme you worked into your debut novel.

The devil is a major character in 'Vaults of Secrets' and 'In the Name of Our Father' largely because the two books deal with human ills and when humans are found wanting, the first thing they do is to look for who to blame. We hardly blame ourselves and in most cases, we blame the devil. The devil is every sinner's fall guy. A man decides to start a church when he has not received the call, he goes to a babalawo to get juju to draw people to his church and he begins to perform fake miracles. How on earth can the devil be responsible for that? It is a conscious decision. We have seen armed robbers blaming the devil for killing their victims after robbing them. This is no devil. It is a conscious decision that no one else but them should be blamed. I think many men and women are worse than the devil they are blaming for their evil deeds. We should be bold enough to accept the responsibility for our errors.

Prophet Jeremiah, the protagonist in 'Angels Live in Heaven', the story-within-story in 'In the Name of Our Father', was not on drugs when he set out to be evil, even Nkechi who wanted to pin a pregnancy on him chose to do so on her own and as such the blame is on them.

The male and female characters in VoS also choose their own paths and the blame should be theirs and not the devil.

Another thing that seems like a motif in the volume is the female narrator/character that keeps secret ranging from infidelity and the paternity of their children. Your female characters seem to be secretive. Anybody applying a feminist critique to the reading might find it troubling. What would you say on that?

There are as much flawed female characters as male characters in this book that anybody applying a feminist critique to the reading should not find it troubling, except the person is just out for fault-finding— which is a different ball game that I cannot help. I respect women and my writing does too. I never set out to have secretive female characters and I know for a fact that the book actually has equal measure of male and female characters that are secretive. So, it will be unfair to accuse me of promoting patriarchy or anything close to that. In the same story where the female character, Dazini, has issues of infidelity and paternity, there is Moses, the man who is her partner in infidelity. No one is guiltier than the other and I know that is clear in the story. The story even shows Dazini's husband, Colonel Edward Dibiana, as egoistic man, who in this time and age still blames a woman for not conceiving. The way he is portrayed is like a protest in support of feminism against patriarchy.

There are many other male characters that are secretive, such as the one who keeps his paternity issue away from his caring wife; there is also Emmanuel, who specialises in helping people to bury their secrets even when it can harm the society; we also have Nelson, who was planning treasonable acts and kept his adorable wife in the dark only for her to suffer as a result of his action; and there is the annoying Nonso whose life is built around secret adventures. I can also remember the annoying Olola Akioye who is impotent but keeps dating women to hide the secret from the society. On a last note, there is also a male character who is used to wipe out a whole family and sets up a law firm from the proceeds and he keeps this secret to himself. Then there is the man caught with his house-help and begging to have the secret hidden from his church and his wife. Sincerely, there are so many secretive men in this book. The female characters are not the only secretive ones.

Another thing I also find distinguishable in the collection is the style adopted in telling the stories. For example, the opening story, 'Till We Meet to Part No More', is written in a monologue and epistolary technique. I would like you to also speak on technique.

I wanted a collection with varieties in terms of techniques and voices. If you don't like first person narrative style, there is second person and if you don't like that also, there is the third person narrative style. Aside the first story, which takes the monologue or epistolary form, there is another story done in a diary form. Personally, I enjoy first person narration because it has a way of making me feel like I am a part of the story and it gives this creative memoir feel that I find alluring and when it now takes the form of epistle or monologue, I find it emotional.

The Almighty technique, also known as the third person narrative technique, makes me feel like God, the all-knowing and helps a writer escape the limitations of the first person narration where the narrator has to witness everything he is writing about or he is a good eavesdropper or someone tells him. The second person narrative style also gives the third person feel. I like it because of the way it makes the reader feel he or she is being addressed.

The last story is particularly striking because it combines elements of first and third person narrative styles because the narrator is Dazini's conscience, which is all-knowing.

Okay, on a lighter note, I wonder if you would be willing to share any secret writing this book? I mean, if you have any secret procedures for writing?

I really do not have any secret procedure for writing. At some point I used to think I needed absolute silence to write. With time I have discovered I can write even when there is some noise, maybe my journalism background is responsible for that because the story must always be delivered no matter the condition. And now I am trying to experiment with writing with music.

Let me also reveal a secret about what eventually became *Vaults of Secrets*. It started as an attempt to do a second novel. I had this idea of doing a novel about three politically-exposed persons who are in jail for treasonable felony. It was to take the form of diaries by each of them about their lives in prison and before prison, but after writing over fifty thousand words, I felt something was missing. I left it for a year or so and when I went back to it, I needed no one to tell me that it would work better as short stories. So, I started working on the script all over again. And another secret, I did not set out to write about secrets, but when I finished, it jumped at me that the theme has forced itself on me and I am glad.

ACKNOWLEDGEMENTS

The stories in *Vaults of Secrets* benefitted from the insights of many people who read the drafts and made brilliant suggestions to turn them around for the better. This confirms that writing is a solitary endeavour but getting a book published is teamwork.

Oluwafemi John Ayodele, my Editor, deserves a special mention for pestering me and asking the right questions. Thanks, Femi for being 'brutal' with the stories. Your courage is the sort I look out for in a fiction Editor.

To Azafi Omoluabi-Ogosi, my Publisher, *e se pupo*! Your touch is remarkable. Thanks for succumbing to my pressure to put the *Azafi* magic on the stories.

Opemipo Rufus Oladipupo, more blessing for obliging me at short notice to read through this when it was yet in its manuscript form. Your observations were important and I worked with them.

To Femi Macaulay, Seun Akioye, Busola Odugbesan, Jane Chijioke and others who I used to gauge an average reader's reaction, thanks for the fresh perspectives. Mr. Macaulay, I thank you for pointing out the defect in *This Special Gift*.

I also thank Mr Sam Omatseye—my wordsmith boss— for his perceptive suggestion on the story that evolved into *This Special Gift*.

Thanks also to Michael Afenfia and Damola Olofinlua for

publishing versions of *Otapiapia*, *This Thing Called Love* and *Lydia's World* on michaelafenfia.com.

To Ayomi, Pempo and The Tones, thanks for helping me form a clan.

And to the Omnipotent and the Omniscient, I owe you all. Without your uncommon grace, I am absolutely nothing.

ABOUT THE AUTHOR

OLUKOREDE SADIQ YISHAU is an Associate Editor with The Nation, a Lagos, Nigeria based newspaper, where he has worked for over a decade.

Yishau, who earlier worked as a journalist with *The Source* and *TELL* magazines, was in 2015 declared Columnist of the Year at the prestigious Nigeria Media Merit Awards (NMMA). That night he was also crowned NMMA Entertainment Reporter of the Year.

Yishau, a graduate of Mass Communication from the Ambrose Alli University, Ekpoma, also has in his kitty honours, such as : NMMA Capital Market Reporter of the Year (2013), NMMA Aviation Industry Reporter of the Year (2003), Finalist, Union Bank's Banking and Finance Reporter of the Year (2003), Finalist, Olu Aboderin Entertainment Reporter of the Year (2001), Finalist, Print Journalist of the Year (2005), and Finalist, Political Reporter of the Year (2006).

His poems were published in an anthology of poetry ACTIVISTS POETS edited by Tunde Oladunjoye in the late 90s. He writes a column ABOVE WHISPERS in The Nation every Friday.

In the Name of Our Father is his debut. He is concluding work on his second novel *Like Someone Skating on Thin Ice*.

Printed in Great Britain
by Amazon